"Are you saying that we slept together and that I am the father of your baby?" he demanded.

She stared wordlessly at him, hurt still crowding viciously into her chest. "Are you trying to say we didn't? That I imagined the weeks we spent together or that you left me without a word and never looked back?"

"I don't remember you," he said hoarsely. "I don't remember any of it. You. Us. That." He gestured toward her belly.

He trailed off and something about the bewilderment in his voice made her stop in her tracks. She crossed her arms protectively over her chest and swallowed.

"You don't remember."

He ran a hand through his hair and swore under his breath. "I had an… accident. Several months ago. I don't remember you. If what you're saying is true, we met during the part of my memory that is a complete blank."

Dear Reader,

This month marks the release of the first book in my new Pregnancy & Passion mini-series for Desire! I'm so excited to bring you the stories of four very powerful men who are brought to their knees by four very special women.

In *Enticed By His Forgotten Lover*, Rafael de Luca makes a very painful discovery about his past actions. Actions that could very well drive away the woman he's fallen hard for.

Rafael and Bryony certainly don't have a smooth path to happily ever after, but it's all the more sweet because love is a very hard-fought victory for these two.

I hope you enjoy their story and that you'll join me for the stories of Rafael's closest friends, Ryan Beardsley, Devon Carter and Cameron Hollingsworth. Nothing about these men is easy, which makes their stories that much more endearing.

Until next time, happy reading!

Love,

Maya Banks

Enticed by His Forgotten Lover

MAYA BANKS

First published in Great Britain 2012
by Mills & Boon, an imprint of Harlequin (UK) Limited.
Large Print edition 2012
Harlequin (UK) Limited,
Eton House, 18-24 Paradise Road,
Richmond, Surrey TW9 1SR

© Maya Banks 2011

ISBN: 978 0 263 22968 4

Harlequin (UK) policy is to use papers that are natural,
renewable and recyclable products and made from
wood grown in sustainable forests. The logging
and manufacturing process conform to the legal
environmental regulations of the country of origin.

Printed and bound in Great Britain
by CPI Antony Rowe, Chippenham, Wiltshire

MAYA BANKS

has loved romance novels from a very (very) early age, and almost from the start, she dreamed of writing them, as well. In her teens she filled countless notebooks with overdramatic stories of love and passion. Today her stories are only slightly less dramatic, but no less romantic.

She lives in Texas with her husband and three children and wouldn't contemplate living anywhere other than the South. When she's not writing, she's usually hunting, fishing or playing poker. She loves to hear from her readers, and she can be found on Facebook (www.facebook.com/pages/Maya-Banks/323801453301?ref=ts) or you can follow her on Twitter (www.twitter.com/maya_banks). Her website, http://www.mayabanks.com is where you can find up to date information on all of Maya's current and forthcoming releases.

To Jane Litte because she loves this
trope above all others ;)

To Charles Griemsman
for all his words of encouragement
and his never-ending patience

<u>One</u>

Rafael de Luca had been in worse situations before, and he'd no doubt be in worse in the future. He could handle it. These people would never make him sweat. They'd never know that he had absolutely no memory of any of them.

He surveyed the crowded ballroom with grim tolerance, sipping at the tasteless wine to cover the fact that he was uneasy. It was only by force of will that he'd managed to last this long. His head was pounding a vicious cadence that made it hard to down the swallow of wine without his stomach heaving it back up.

"Rafe, you can pack it in," Devon Carter murmured next to him. "You've put in enough time. No one suspects a thing."

Rafael swiveled to see his three friends—Devon, Ryan Beardsley and Cameron Hollingsworth—standing protectively at his back. There was significance there. Always at his back. Ever since they were freshmen in college, determined to make their mark on the business world.

They had come when he was lying in the hospital, a yawning black hole in his memory. They hadn't coddled him. Quite the opposite. They'd been complete bastards. He was still grateful for that.

"I've been told I never leave a party early," Rafe said as he tipped the wine toward his mouth again. As soon as the aroma wafted through his nostrils, he lowered the glass, changing his mind. What he wouldn't give for a bloody painkiller.

He'd refused any medication. He despised how out of control painkillers made him feel. But right now, he'd gladly take a few and pass out for several hours. Maybe then he'd wake up without the god-awful pain in his temples.

Cam's lips twisted in a half snarl. "Who gives a damn what you typically do? It's your party. Tell them all to—"

Ryan held up his hand. "They're important business associates, Cam. We want their money, remember?"

Cam scowled as he scanned the room.

"Who needs a security team with the three of you around?" Rafael drawled. He joked, but he was grateful for people he could trust. There was no one else he'd admit his memory loss to.

Devon leaned in quickly and said in a low voice, "The man approaching is Quenton Ramsey the third. His wife's name is Marcy. He's already confirmed for the Moon Island deal."

Rafael nodded and took a step away from the shelter of his friends and smiled warmly at the approaching couple. A lot rode on making sure their investors didn't get nervous. Rafael and his business partners had located a prime spot for their resort—a tiny island off the coast of Texas just across the bay from Galveston. The land was his. Now all they had to do was build the hotel and keep their investors happy.

"Quenton, Marcy, it's wonderful to see you both again. And may I say how lovely you look tonight, Marcy. Quenton is a very lucky man."

The older woman's cheeks flushed with pleasure as Rafael took her hand and brought it to his lips.

He nodded politely and pretended interest in the couple, but his nape was prickling again, and he squelched the urge to rub it. His head was lowered as if he were hanging on to every word, but his gaze rapidly took in the room, searching for the source of his unease.

At first his gaze flickered past her but he yanked his attention back to the woman standing across the room. Her stare bore holes through him. Unflinching and steady even when his eyes locked with hers.

It was hard for him to discern why he was so arrested by her. He knew he generally preferred tall, leggy blondes. He was a total sucker for baby blues and soft, pale skin.

This woman was petite, even in heels, and had a creamy olive complexion. A wealth of inky black curls cascaded over her shoulders and her eyes were equally dark.

She looked at him as if she'd already judged him and found him lacking. He'd never seen her before in his life. Or had he?

He cursed the gaping hole in his memory. He remembered nothing of the weeks before his accident four months ago and had gaps in his memory preceding the weeks that he remembered nothing of. It was all so…random. Selective amnesia. It was complete and utter bull. No one got amnesia except hysterical women in bad soap operas. His physician suggested that there was a psychological reason for the missing pieces of his memory. Rafael hadn't appreciated such a suggestion. He wasn't crazy. Who the hell *wanted* to lose their memory?

He remembered Dev, Cam and Ryan. Every moment of the past decade. Their years in college. Their success in business. He remembered most of the people who worked for him. Most. But not all, which caused him no end of stress in his offices. Especially since he was trying to close a resort development deal that could make him and his partners millions.

Now he was stuck not remembering who half his investors were and he couldn't afford to lose anyone at this stage of the game.

The woman was still staring at him, but she'd made no move to approach him. Her eyes had grown colder the longer their gazes held, and her hand tightened perceptibly on her small clutch.

"Excuse me," he murmured to the Ramseys.

With a smooth smile, he disengaged himself from the group who'd assembled around him and discreetly made his way in the direction of his mystery woman.

His security team followed at a short distance, but he ignored them. They didn't shadow him for fear of his safety as much as his partners feared it getting out that he'd lost his memory. The security team was an annoyance he was unused to, but they kept people at arm's length, which served him well at the moment.

The woman didn't pretend to be coy. She stared straight at him and as he approached, her chin thrust upward in a gesture of defiance that intrigued him.

For a moment he stood in front of her, studying the delicate lines of her face and wondering if in fact this was their first meeting. Surely he would have remembered.

"Excuse me, but have we met?" he asked in his smoothest voice, one that he knew to be particularly effective on women.

Likely she'd titter and then deny such a meeting. Or she'd blatantly lie and try to convince him that they'd spent a wonderful night in bed.

Which he knew couldn't be true, because she wasn't his type.

His gaze settled over the generous swell of her breasts pushed up by the empire waist of her black cocktail dress. The rest of the dress fell in a swirl to her knees and twitched with sudden impatience.

She did none of the things he'd supposed. When he glanced back up at her face, he saw fury reflected in the dark pools of her eyes.

"*Met?* Have we *met?*" Her voice was barely above a whisper, but he felt each word like the crack of a whip. "You sorry bastard!"

Before he could process the shock of her outburst she nailed him with a right hook. He stumbled back, holding his nose.

"Son of a—"

Before he could demand to know if she'd lost her damn mind, one of his guards stepped between him and the woman, and in the confusion accidentally sent her reeling backward. She stumbled and went down on one knee, her hand automatically flying to the folds of her dress.

It was then, as she cupped her belly, that the realization hit him. The folds had hidden the gentle curve of her body. Had hidden her pregnancy and the evidence of a child.

His guard went to roughly haul her to her feet.

"No!" Rafael roared. "She's pregnant. Do not hurt her!"

His guard stepped back, his startled gaze going to Rafael. The woman wasted no time scrambling to her feet. Her eyes flashing, she turned and ran down the marble hallway, her heels tapping a loud staccato as she fled.

Rafael stared at her retreating figure, too stunned to do or say anything. The last time she'd looked at him, it wasn't fury he'd seen. It wasn't the fiery anger that prompted her to hit him. No, he'd seen tears and hurt. Somehow, he'd hurt this woman and damned if he knew how.

The vicious ache in his head forgotten, he hurried down the hallway after her. He burst from the hotel lobby, and when he reached the steps leading down to the busy streets, he saw two shoes sparkling in the moonlight, the silvery glitter twinkling at him. Mocking him.

He bent and picked up the strappy sandals and then he frowned. A pregnant woman had no business wearing heels this high. What if she'd tripped and fallen? Why the devil had she run? It certainly seemed as if she wanted a confrontation with him, but at first opportunity, she'd fled.

At least she'd had the common sense to ditch them so she wasn't running down some street on a pair of toothpicks.

"What the hell is going on, Rafe?" Cam demanded as he hurried up behind him.

In fact, his entire security team, along with Cam, Ryan and Devon, had followed him from the hotel into the crisp autumn air. Now they gathered around him and they looked as though they were concerned. About him.

He blew out his breath in frustration and then shoved the pair of sparkly, ultra-feminine shoes at Ramon, his head of security.

"Find the woman who wore these shoes."

"What would you like me to do with her when I find her?" Ramon asked in a sober voice that told Rafael he'd definitely find the woman in short order. Ramon didn't typically fail in any task Rafael set him to.

Rafael shook his head. "You aren't to do anything. Report back to me. I'll handle the situation."

He was treated to a multitude of frowns.

"I don't like it, Rafe," Ryan said. "This screams

setup. It's not impossible that your memory loss hasn't already been leaked to the press or even a few confidential sources who haven't yet gone wide with it. A woman could manipulate you in a thousand ways by using it against you."

"Yes, she could," Rafael said calmly. "There's something about this woman that bugs me, though."

Cam's brow lifted in that imperious way that intimidated so many people. "Do you recognize her? Is she someone you knew?"

Rafael frowned. "I don't know. Yet. But I'm going to find out."

Bryony Morgan stepped from the shower, wrapped a towel around her head and then pulled on a robe. Even a warm shower hadn't stopped the rapid thump of her pulse. Try as she might, she hadn't been able to let go of her rage.

Have we met?

His question replayed over and over until she wanted to throw something. Preferably at him.

How could she have been so stupid? She wasn't typically one to lose her mind over a good-looking man. She'd been immune to a good many with charm and wit.

But from the time Rafael de Luca had stepped onto her island, he'd been it for her. No fighting. No resisting. He was the entire package. Perfection in those uptight business suits he wore. Oh, she'd managed to get them off of him. By the time he left the island, his pilot hadn't even recognized him.

He'd gone from a sober, uptight, type A personality to laid-back, relaxed and well vacationed.

And in love.

She closed her eyes against the sudden surge of pain that swamped her.

He obviously hadn't been in love. Or anything else. He came. He saw. And he conquered. She was just too hopelessly naive and too in love herself to consider his true motives.

That may well have been the case, but it didn't mean he was going to get away scot-free with his lies and deception. She didn't care what she had to do, he wasn't going to develop the land she'd sold him into some ginormous tourist mecca and turn the entire island into some playground for bored, wealthy jet-setters.

It had taken all her courage to crash his party tonight, but once she'd learned the purpose—a gathering of his potential investors for the project he planned to ruin her land with—she'd been determined to confront him. Right there in their midst. Daring him to lie to her when the entire room knew of his plans.

She hadn't counted on him denying that he'd ever met her. But then how better to paint her as the village idiot? Or some crazy do-gooder granola bar out to halt "progress."

The force of just how wrong she'd been threatened to flatten her. She sighed heavily and shook her head. She had to calm down or her blood pressure was going to skyrocket.

Slowly she unclenched her jaw. Her teeth were ground together with enough force to break them.

Where was room service? She was starving. She rubbed her belly apologetically and made a conscious effort to let all the anger and stress flow out of her body. It couldn't be good for the baby to have her mother so pissed off all the time.

She gritted her teeth before she realized that she'd done so again. Forcing her jaw to relax once more, she performed the arduous task of combing out her hair and blow-drying it.

She was finishing up when a loud knock sounded at her door.

"Food. Finally," she murmured as she turned off the hair dryer.

She hurried to the door and swung it open. But there was no food cart or hotel employee. Rafael stood there, her abandoned shoes dangling from his fingertips.

She stepped back and tried to slam the door, but he stuck his foot in, preventing her from shutting it.

As indomitable as ever, he pushed his way in and stood in front of her. She hated how small and vulnerable she felt against him. Oh, she hadn't always hated it. She'd loved how protected and cherished he'd made her feel when she curled her much smaller body into his.

She bared her teeth into a snarl. "Get out or I'll call hotel security."

"You could," he said calmly. "But as I own this hotel, you might have a hard time having me thrown out."

Her eyes narrowed. Of course he'd own the hotel she'd chosen to stay in. What were the odds of that?

"I'll call the police then. I don't care who you are. You can't force yourself into my hotel room."

He raised an eyebrow. "I came to return your shoes. Does that make me a criminal?"

"Oh, come on, Rafael! Stop playing stupid games. It's beneath you. Or it should be. I get it. Believe me—I get it! I got it as soon as you looked right through me at the party. Though I have to say, the 'have we met?' line? That was priceless. Just priceless. Not to mention overkill."

It was all she could do not to hit him again, and maybe he realized just how badly she wanted to because he took a wary step back.

She advanced, not willing for a moment to allow him to control the situation. "You know what? I never took you for a coward. You played me. I get that. I was a monumental idiot. But for you to hide from the inevitable confrontation like you've done makes me physically ill."

She stuck a finger into his chest, ignoring the baffled look on his face. "Furthermore, you're not going to get away with your plans for *my* land. If it takes every cent I own, I'll fight you. We had a verbal agreement, and you'll stick to it."

He blinked, then looked as if he was about to say something.

She crossed her arms, so furious she wanted to

kick him. If it wouldn't land her on her ass, she'd do it.

"What? Did you think you'd never see me again? That I'd hide away somewhere and sulk because I learned you don't really love me and slept with me to get me to agree to sell to you? You couldn't be more mistaken," she seethed.

Rafael reacted as though she'd hit him again. His face paled and his eyes became hard, cold points. If she weren't so angry, what she saw in his gaze would probably scare the bejesus out of her. But Mamaw had always said that common sense was the first thing to go when someone got all riled up. Boy, was that the truth.

"Are you trying to insinuate that you and I have slept together?" he asked in a dangerously low voice that—again—should have frightened her. But she was way beyond fear. "I don't even know your name."

It shouldn't have hurt her. She'd long since realized why Rafael had chosen her. Why he'd seduced her and why he'd told her the lies he told. He couldn't shoulder the entire blame. She'd been far too easy a conquest.

But still, that he'd stand there before her and categorically deny even knowing her name sliced a jagged line through her heart that was beyond repair.

"You should go," she said in a barely controlled tone. Damn the tears, but if he didn't leave now, she wasn't going to keep her composure for long.

His brow furrowed and he cocked his head to the side, studying her intently. Then to her dismay, he swept his hand out and smudged a tear from the corner of her eye with his thumb.

"You're upset."

Sweet mother of God, this man was an idiot. She could only pray their child inherited her brains and not his. She nearly laughed aloud but it came out as a strangled sob. How could she hope for the poor baby to inherit any intelligence whatsoever when it was clear that both his parents were flaming morons?

"Get. Out."

But instead he cupped her chin and tilted it upward so he could stare into her eyes. Then he wiped at the dampness on her cheek in a surprisingly gentle gesture.

"We can't have slept together. Besides the fact that you aren't my type, I can't imagine forgetting such an event."

Her mouth gaped open and any thoughts of

tears fled. She wrenched herself from his grasp and gave up trying to get the man out of her room. He could stay. She was going.

She gripped the lapels of her robe and stomped around him. She made it into the hall before his hand closed around her wrist and he pulled her up short.

Enough was enough. She opened her mouth to let out a shriek, but he yanked her against his hard body and covered her mouth.

"For God's sake, I'm not going to hurt you," he hissed.

He muscled her back into the hotel room, slammed the door and bolted it shut behind them. Then he turned and glared at her.

"You've already hurt me," she said through gritted teeth.

His eyes softened and grew cloudy with confusion.

"It's obvious you feel as though I've wronged you in some way. I'd apologize, but I'd have to remember you and what I supposedly did in order to offer restitution."

"Restitution?" She gaped at him, stunned by the difference in the Rafael de Luca she fell in love with and this man standing before her now. She yanked open her robe so that the small mound of her belly showed through the thin, satin night-gown underneath. "You make me fall in love with you. You seduce me. You tell me you love me and that you want us to be together. You get my signature on papers agreeing to sell you land that has been in my family for a century. You feed me complete lies about our relationship and your plans for the land. But that wasn't enough. No, you had to get me pregnant on top of it all!"

His face went white. Anger removed all the confusion from his features. He took a step toward her and for the first time, fear edged out her fury. She took a step back and braced her hand against the TV stand.

"Are you saying that we slept together and that I am the father of your baby?" he demanded.

She stared wordlessly at him, hurt still crowding viciously into her chest. "Are you trying to say we didn't? That I imagined the weeks we spent together? Do you deny that you left me without a word and never looked back?"

Sarcasm crept into her voice but there was also deep pain that she wished wasn't so evident. It was enough that he'd betrayed her. She didn't want to be humiliated further.

He flinched and closed his eyes. Then he took a step back and for a moment she thought he was finally going to do as she'd demanded and leave.

"I don't remember you," he said hoarsely. "I don't remember any of it. You. Us. That." He gestured toward her belly.

He trailed off and something about the bewilderment in his voice made her stop in her tracks. She crossed her arms protectively over her chest and swallowed.

"You don't remember."

He ran a hand through his hair and swore under his breath. "I had an…accident. Several months ago. I don't remember you. If what you're saying is true, we met during the period where my memory is a complete blank."

Two

Rafael watched as all the color leeched from her face and she swayed unsteadily. With a curse, he reached to grasp her arms. This time she didn't fight him. She was limp in his hands and he felt the slight tremble beneath his fingers.

"Come, sit down, before you fall," he said grimly.

He led her to the bed and she sat, her hands going to the edge to brace herself.

She glanced up at him, her eyes haunted. "You expect me to believe you have *amnesia?* Is that the best you could come up with?"

He winced because he felt much the same about the idea of amnesia. If all she'd said was true and their positions were reversed, he'd laugh her out of the room.

"I don't ask this to make you angry, but what is your name? I feel at quite a disadvantage here."

She sighed and rubbed a hand wearily through her thick hair. "You're serious about this."

He made a sound of impatience and she pinched the bridge of her nose between her fingers.

"My name is Bryony Morgan," she said quietly.

She bowed her head and black curls fell forward, hiding her profile. Unable to resist, he ran his finger over her cheek and then pushed the hair back behind her ear.

"Well, Bryony, it would seem you and I have a lot to discuss. I have many, many questions as you can well imagine."

She turned her head to stare up at him. "Amnesia. You're seriously going to stick to this insane story?"

He tried to remember how skeptical he'd be in her shoes, but her outright disbelief was ticking him off. He wasn't used to having his word questioned by anyone.

"Do you think I like being punched in the face at a public gathering by a woman claiming to be pregnant with my child when to my knowledge it's the first time we've met? Put yourself in my shoes for a moment. If a man you'd never seen before or had no memory of walked up to you and said the things to you that you're saying to me, don't you think you'd be a little suspicious? Hell, you'd probably have already called the cops you keep threatening me with."

"This is crazy," she muttered.

"Look, I can prove what happened to me. I can show you my medical records and the doctor's diagnosis. I don't remember you, Bryony. I'm sorry if that hurts you, but it's a fact. I have only your word that we were ever anything to each other."

Her lips twisted. "Yeah, we can't forget I'm not your type."

He winced. Trust her to remember that remark.

"I'd like for you to tell me everything. Start from the beginning. Tell me when and where we met. Maybe something you say will jog my memory."

A knock sounded at the door and he scowled. "Are you expecting someone at this hour?" he asked when she rose to answer it.

"Room service. I'm starving. I haven't eaten all day."

"That can't be good for the baby."

She didn't look as though she appreciated the remark. Gathering her robe tighter around her, she went to the door and a few seconds later, a room service attendant wheeled in a cart bearing covered plates. She signed the bill and offered a halfhearted smile of thanks to the man.

When Rafael and Bryony were alone again she pushed the cart the rest of the way to the bed. "Sorry. Obviously I wasn't counting on company. I only ordered enough food for one."

He lifted a brow as she began uncovering the dishes. There was enough food to feed a small convention.

"Sit down and relax. We can talk while you're eating."

She settled in the armchair catty-corner to the bed and curled her feet underneath her. As she reached for one of the plates, he studied the face of the woman he'd forgotten.

She was beautiful. No denying that. Not the kind of woman he usually gravitated toward. She was entirely too outspoken for his liking. He preferred women who were gentle and, according to his close friends, submissive.

Quite frankly it made him sound like a jackass.

But he couldn't deny he did like his women a bit more biddable. He found it fascinating that he'd supposedly met and fallen in love with Bryony Morgan, the antithesis of every woman he'd dated for the past five years.

Okay, so he bought that he'd been attracted to her. And yeah, he could buy sleeping with her. But falling in love? In a span of a few weeks?

That was a giant hole in the fairy tale she'd spun.

But she was also a woman, and women tended to be emotional creatures. It was possible she thought he was in love with her. Her hurt and betrayal certainly didn't seem feigned.

And then there was the fact she was pregnant with his child. It would probably make him seem even more of a bastard, but it would be stupid not to insist on paternity testing. It wasn't out of the realm of possibility that she'd made the entire thing up after learning of his memory loss.

He had the sudden urge to call his lawyer and have him tell him whose signature was on the real estate contract for the land he'd purchased sometime during the weeks he'd lost. He hadn't seen the paperwork since before his accident. He paid people to keep his business running and his affairs in order. Once he scored the deal, there was no reason to look back.

Until now.

Damn but this was a mess. And yeah, he was definitely calling his lawyer first thing in the morning.

"What are you thinking?" she asked bluntly.

"That this is a huge cluster f—"

"You're telling me," she muttered. "Only I don't see what's so bad from your perspective. You've got more money than God. You're not pregnant, and you didn't just sign away land that's been in your family for generations to a man who's going to destroy it to build some tourist trap."

The pain in her voice sent an uncomfortable sensation through his chest. Something remarkably like guilt ate at him, but what did he have to feel guilty about? None of this was his fault.

"How did we meet?" he asked. "I need to know everything."

She toyed with her fork, and her lips turned down into an unhappy frown.

"The first time I saw you, you were wearing an uptight suit, shoes that cost more than my house and you had on sunglasses. It annoyed me that I couldn't see your eyes, so I refused to speak to you until you took them off."

"And where was this?"

"Moon Island. You were asking about a stretch of beachfront property and who owned it. I, of course, was the owner, and I figured you were some guy from the city with big plans to develop the island and save all the locals from a life of poverty."

He frowned. "It wasn't for sale? I remember it being for sale before I ever went down there. I wouldn't have known about it otherwise."

She nodded. "It was. I…I needed to sell it. My grandmother and I could no longer afford the property taxes. But we agreed we wouldn't sell to a developer. It was bad enough that I was forced to sell land that's been in my family for generations."

She broke off, clearly uncomfortable with all she'd shared.

"Anyway, I figured you for another stiff suit, and so I sent you across the island on a wild-goose chase."

He sent a glare in her direction. For the first time, a smile flirted on the edge of her lips.

"You were so angry with me. You stormed back

to my cottage and banged on my door. You demanded to know what the hell I was doing and said I didn't act like someone who desperately needed to sell a piece of land."

"That sounds like me," he acknowledged.

"I informed you that I wasn't interested in selling to you and you demanded to know why. When I told you of my promise to my grandmother that we'd only sell to someone willing to sign a guarantee that they wouldn't commercially develop the stretch of beach, you asked to meet her."

An uncomfortable prickle went up his nape. That didn't sound like him. He wasn't one to get personal. Everyone had their price. He would have simply upped his offer until he found theirs.

"The rest is pretty embarrassing," she said lightly. "I took you to meet Mamaw. The two of you got along famously. She invited you to stay for supper. Afterward we took a walk on the beach. You kissed me. I kissed you back. You walked me back to my cottage and told me you'd see me the next day."

"And did I?"

"Oh, yes," she whispered. "And the day after,

and the day after. It took me three days to talk you out of that suit."

He lifted a brow and stared.

Her cheeks turned red and she clamped a hand over her mouth. "Oh, God, I didn't mean it like that. You wore that suit everywhere on the beach. You stuck out like a sore thumb. So I took you shopping. We bought you beachwear."

This was starting to sound like a nightmare. "Beachwear?"

Her head bobbed up and down. "Shorts. T-shirts. Flip-flops."

Maybe the doctor had been right. He lost his memory because he *wanted* to forget. Flip-flops? It was all he could do not to stare down at his very expensive leather loafers and imagine wearing flip-flops.

"And I wore this…beachwear."

She raised an eyebrow. "You did. We bought swim trunks, too. I don't know of anyone who goes to an island and doesn't pack something to swim in, so we got you some trunks and I took you to my favorite stretch of the beach."

So far her version of the weeks missing from his memory was so divergent from everything he knew of himself that it was like listening to a story about someone else. What could have possessed him to act so out of character?

"How long did this relationship you say we had go on?" he croaked.

"Four weeks," she said softly. "Four wonderful weeks. We were together every day. By the end of the first week, you gave up your hotel room and you stayed with me. In my bed. We'd make love with the windows open so we could listen to the ocean."

"I see."

Her eyes narrowed. "You don't believe me."

"Bryony," he said carefully. "This is very difficult for me. I'm missing a month of my life and what you're telling me sounds so fantastical, so utterly out of character for me, that I can't even wrap my head around it."

She pressed her lips together but he could still see them tremble. "Yeah, I get that this is difficult for you. But try to see things from my perspective for just a few moments. Imagine that the person you were in love with and thought was in love with you suddenly can't remember you. Imagine what kind of doubts you have when you discover that everything he told you was a lie and that he made you promises he didn't keep. How would you feel?"

He stared into her eyes, gutted by the sorrow he saw. "I'd be pretty damn upset."

"Yeah. That about covers it."

She stood and pushed the serving cart back so that she could step around it. Her hand crept around the back of her neck and she rubbed absently as she stood just a short distance from where he sat on the edge of the bed.

"Look, this is…pointless. I'm really tired. You should probably go now."

He shot to his feet. "You want me to go?" It was on the tip of his tongue to ask her if she was out of her damn mind, but that wouldn't win him any more points with her. "After dumping this story on me, after telling me I'm going to be a father, you expect me to just walk away?"

"It's what you did before," she said wearily.

"How the hell can you say that? How do you know what I did or didn't do when *I* don't even know? You said you loved me and that I loved you. I've just told you I can't remember any of it. How do you get that I walked away from you? That I somehow betrayed you? I was in an accident, Bryony. What was the last day you saw me? What did we do? Did I dump you? Did I tell you I was leaving you?"

Her face was white and her fingers were balled into tiny fists at her sides.

"It was the day after we closed on the land. You said you had to go back to New York. It was some emergency you had to attend to personally. You said it wouldn't take more than a day or two. You told me you'd be back, that you couldn't wait to come back, and that once you'd returned, we'd discuss what we'd do with the land," she said painfully.

"What day was it? The date, Bryony. The exact date."

"June third."

"The day of my accident."

She looked stricken. Her hand flew to her mouth. She looked so unsteady that he thought she might fall. He reached out, snagged her wrist and pulled her down to sit beside him. She didn't fight. She just stared at him numbly.

"How? What happened?"

"My private jet went down over Kentucky," he said grimly. "I don't remember a lot. I woke up in a hospital and had no idea how I'd come to be there."

"And you remember nothing?" she asked hoarsely.

"Only those four weeks. I have some other gaps but it's mostly people I'm supposed to know or remember but don't. I didn't initially remember the circumstances surrounding my decision to fly down to Moon Island, but that's easy enough to figure out since I bought a piece of property while I was there."

"So you just forgot *me,*" she said with a forced laugh.

He sighed. "I know it's not easy to hear. Try to understand that I'm having the same difficulty believing all you've told me. I may not remember you, Bryony, but I'm not a complete bastard. It doesn't bring me any satisfaction to see how much this hurts you."

"I tried to call," she said bleakly. "At first I waited. I told myself all sorts of excuses. It was a bigger emergency. You're a really busy guy. But then I tried to call the number you'd given me. No one would let me speak to you. There were always excuses. You were in a meeting. You were out of town. You were at lunch."

"There was a pretty tight security net around me after the accident. We didn't want anyone to know of my memory loss. We were afraid it would make investors lose their confidence in me. Any sign of weakness will make many people pull out of a deal."

"It looked—and felt—like a brush-off, and it pissed me off the more time that passed because you didn't have the balls to tell me to my face."

"So why now? Why did you wait so long to come here and confront me?"

She stared warily at him as if determining whether he was suspicious of her motives. And maybe he was. It certainly made sense that if she'd been that angry—and pregnant—she wouldn't have waited four months to confront him.

"I didn't find out I was pregnant until I was nearly ten weeks along. And Mamaw was having health problems so I was spending a lot of time with her. I didn't want to upset her by telling her that I suspected you'd seduced me and lied to me—to us—about your plans for the land. It would have broken her heart. Not just about the land. She knew how much I loved you. She wanted me happy."

Well, damn. He felt about two inches tall.

He ran a hand through his hair and wondered

how the hell someone's life could change so drastically in a single day.

"We have some decisions to make, Bryony."

She turned and tilted her head in his direction. "Decisions?"

He met her gaze. "You've told me that I was in love with you. That you were in love with me. You've also said that you're pregnant with my child. If you think I'm just going to walk out of your hotel room and not look back, you're insane. We have a hell of a lot to work out and it isn't going to be resolved in a single night. Or day. Or week even."

She nodded her agreement.

"I want you to come with me."

Her eyes widened. Her mouth parted and her tongue swept nervously over her bottom lip.

"Where exactly are we going?"

"If everything you say is true, then a hell of a lot of my life and future changed on that island. You and I are going to go back to where it all started."

She stared in bewilderment at him. Had she expected him to walk away? He wasn't sure if he was angry or resigned over that fact.

"We're going to relive those weeks, Bryony. Maybe being there will bring it all back."

"And if it doesn't?" she asked cautiously.

"Then we'll have spent a lot of time getting reacquainted."

Three

"Have you lost your mind?" Ryan demanded.

Rafael stopped pacing and leveled a stare at his friends, who'd gathered in his office.

"Let's not talk about who's lost their mind," Rafael said pointedly. "I'm not the one mounting a search for the woman who screwed me over with my brother."

Ryan glared at him then shoved his hands into his pockets and turned to stare out the window.

"Low blow," Devon murmured.

Rafael blew out his breath. Yeah, it had been. Whatever the reason for Ryan trying to track down his ex-fiancée, he didn't deserve Rafael acting like an ass.

"Sorry, man," Rafael offered.

Cam leaned back in Rafael's executive chair and placed his feet up on the desk. "I think you're both certifiable. No woman is worth this much trouble." He clasped his hands behind his head and leveled a stare in Rafael's direction. "And you. I don't even know what to say to your crazy idea of going back with her to Moon Island. What do you hope to accomplish?"

That was a damn good question. He wasn't entirely certain. He wanted his memory back. He wanted to know what had made him go off his rocker and supposedly fall in love with and impregnate a woman in a matter of weeks.

He was thirty-four years old, but from all accounts, he'd acted like a teenager faced with his first naked woman.

"She says we fell in love."

He nearly groaned. Just saying the words made him feel utterly ridiculous.

The three other men stared at him as if he'd just announced he was taking a vow of celibacy. Though at the moment, it didn't sound like a bad idea.

"She also claims the child she's pregnant with

is yours," Devon pointed out. "That's a lot of things she's claiming."

"Have you talked to your lawyer?" Ryan asked. "This entire situation makes me nervous. She could do a lot of damage to this deal if she goes public. If she spills her tale of you being a complete bastard, knocking her up and hauling ass before the ink on the contracts was dry, it's not going to make any of us look good."

"No, I damn well haven't spoken to Mario yet," Rafael muttered. "When have I had time? I'm calling him next."

"So how long are you going to be gone on this soul-searching expedition?" Cam asked.

Rafael shoved his hands into his pockets and rocked back on his heels. "As long as it takes."

Devon glanced down at his watch. "As much as I'd love to stick around and be amused by all this, I have an appointment."

"Copeland?" Cam smirked.

Devon curled his lip in Cam's direction.

"The old man still adamant that you marry his daughter if you want the merger?" Ryan asked.

Devon sighed. "Yeah. She's…flighty, and Copeland seems to think I'd settle her."

Rafael winced and shot his friend a look of sympathy.

Cam shrugged. "So tell him the deal's off."

"She's not that bad. She's just young and…exuberant. There are worse women to marry."

"In other words, she'd drive a stick-in-the-mud like you crazy," Ryan said with a grin.

Devon made a rude gesture as he headed toward the door.

Cam swiveled in Rafael's chair and let his feet hit the floor with a thud. "I'm off, too. Make damn sure you give us a heads-up before you head off to find yourself, Rafe."

Rafael grunted and claimed his chair as Cam followed behind Devon. Ryan still stood at the window and he turned to Rafael once they were alone.

"Hey, I'm sorry for the crack about Kelly," Rafael said before Ryan could speak. "Have you been able to find her yet?"

Ryan shook his head. "No. But I will."

Rafael didn't understand Ryan's determination to hunt down his ex-fiancée. The whole fiasco had taken place during the four weeks Rafael had lost, but Devon and Cam had told him that Kelly had slept with Ryan's brother. Ryan had tossed her out and had seemingly moved on. Only now Ryan had hired an investigator to find her.

"You don't remember Bryony?" Ryan asked. "Nothing at all?"

Rafael slapped a pen against the edge of his desk. "No. Nothing. It's like looking at a stranger."

"And you don't think that's odd?"

Rafael made a sound of exasperation. "Well, of course it's odd. Everything about this situation is odd."

Ryan leaned back against the window and studied Rafael. "You'd think if you'd fallen head-over-ass for this woman, spent every waking moment for four weeks with her and managed to knock her up in the process that there would at least be some serious déjà vu."

Rafael tossed the pen down and spun in his chair until his foot caught on the trash can next to his desk. "I get where you're going with this, Ryan, and I appreciate your concern. Something happened on that island. I don't know what, but there is a gaping hole in my memory and she's at the center. I've got to go back, if for no other reason than to disprove her story."

"And if she's telling the truth?" Ryan asked.

"Then I've got a hell of a lot of catching up to do," Rafael muttered.

Bryony stood outside the high-rise office building and stared straight up. The sleek modern architecture glistened in the bright autumn sun. The sky provided a dramatic backdrop as the spire punched a hole in the vivid blue splash.

An orange leaf drifted lazily onto her face, brushing her nose before fluttering to the ground. It joined others on the sidewalk and skittered along the concrete until it was crunched beneath the feet of the many passersby.

She was jostled by someone shouldering past her and she heard a muttered "Tourist" as they hurried on by.

The city frightened and fascinated her in equal parts. Everyone was so busy here. No one stopped even for a moment. The city pulsed with people, cars, lights and noise. Constant noise.

How did anyone stand it?

And yet she'd been ready to embrace it. She'd known that if she were to have a life with Rafael, she'd have to grow used to city life. It was where he lived and worked. Where he thrived.

Now she stood in front of his office building feeling hesitant and insecure. There was a seed of doubt and it grew with each breath. She couldn't help but wonder if she wasn't being an even bigger fool this time.

"Fool me once, blah blah," she muttered. "I must be insane to trust him."

But if he were telling the truth. If his utterly bizarre and improbable story were true, then he hadn't betrayed her. He hadn't dumped her. He hadn't done any of the things she'd accused him of.

Part of her was relieved and the other part had no idea what to think or believe.

"Bryony, is it?"

She yanked her gaze downward, embarrassed that she was still standing in front of the building looking straight up like a moron, and saw two of the men she'd seen with Rafael at the party.

She took a wary step back. "I'm Bryony, yes."

They were both tall. One had medium brown hair, short and neat. He smiled at her. The other one had blond hair with varying shades of brown. It was longish and unruly. He frowned at her, and his blue eyes narrowed as though she were a nasty bug.

The smiling one stuck out his hand. "I'm Devon

Carter, a friend of Rafael's. This is Cameron Hollingsworth."

Cameron continued to scrutinize her so she ignored him and focused on Devon, although she had no idea what to say.

"Nice to meet you," she murmured.

"Are you here to see Rafe?" Devon asked.

She nodded.

"We'll be happy to take you up."

She shook her head. "No, that's okay. I can make it. I mean I don't want to be a bother."

Cameron shot her a cool, assessing look that made her feel vastly inferior. Her chin automatically went up and her fingers balled into a fist at her side. She really wasn't a violent person. Truly. But in the past few days, she'd had her share of violent fantasies. Right now she visualized Cameron Hollingsworth picking himself up off the pavement.

"It's no bother," Devon said smoothly. "The least I can do is see you to the elevator."

She frowned. "You think I'm incapable of finding the elevator? Or are you just one of those really nosy friends?"

Devon's smile was lazy and unbothered. He looked at her as if he knew exactly how wound up she was and that her stomach was in knots. Maybe she had that beautiful look of a woman about to puke.

"Then I'll bid you a good day," Devon finally said.

She swallowed, wishing she hadn't been quite so rude. It was a fault of hers that she went on the offensive the minute she felt at a disadvantage. She wasn't going to win any friends acting like a bitch.

"Thank you. It was nice to meet you."

She injected enough sincerity into her tone that even she believed herself. Devon nodded but Cameron didn't look impressed. She forced herself not to scowl at him as the two men walked to the street and got into a waiting BMW.

Taking a deep breath, she headed to the revolving door and entered the building. The lobby was beautiful. A study in marble and exposed beams. The contrast between old and modern should have looked odd, but instead it looked opulent and rich.

There was a large fountain in the middle of the lobby and she paused to allow the sound of the water to soothe her. She missed the ocean. She didn't venture off the island often, and it made her anxious now, in the midst of so much hustle and bustle, to return to the peace and quiet of the small coastal island she'd grown up on.

Her throat tightened and pain squeezed at her chest. Because of her, her family's land was now in the hands of a man determined to build a resort, golf course and God knew what else. Not that those were bad things. She had nothing against progress. And she certainly wasn't opposed to free enterprise and capitalism. A buck was a buck. Everyone wanted to make a few. Not that Rafael seemed to have any problem in that area.

But Moon Island was special. It was still untouched by the heavy hand of development. The families that lived there had been there for generations. Everyone knew everyone else. Half the island fished or shrimped and the other half had retired to the island after working thirty years in cities like Houston or Dallas.

There was an unspoken agreement among the residents that they wanted the island to remain as it was. A quiet place of splendor. A haven for people wanting to get away from life in the fast lane. Things just moved slower there.

Now because of her, that would all change.

Bulldozers and construction crews would move in, and slowly the outside world would creep in and change the way of life.

She bit her lip and turned in the direction of the elevator. It hurt to think how naive she'd been. And now that she had distance from the whirlwind relationship she'd jumped into with Rafael, she knew how stupid she'd been. But at the time… At the time she hadn't been thinking straight. She'd been powerless under his onslaught, his magnetism and the idea that he was as caught up as she was.

She angrily jabbed the button for the thirty-first floor then stepped back as others crowded in. It wasn't as if the thought hadn't occurred to her to add in a legal clause to the contract, but she'd imagined that it would seem as though she didn't trust him. Sort of like demanding a prenuptial agreement before marriage. Yeah, it was smart, but it was also awkward and brought up questions she hadn't wanted at the time.

He'd absolutely sold her on the idea that he wanted to buy the land for personal use. It hadn't been a corporation name on the closing documents. It had been his and only his. Rafael de Luca. And she'd believed him when he'd said he'd be back. That he loved her. That he wanted them to be together.

She was so deeply humiliated over her stupidity that she couldn't bear to think about it. Now, when she'd come to New York to confront Rafael over his lies, she was confronted by his extraordinary claim that he'd lost his memory. It was so damn convenient.

But she couldn't help whispering, "Please let him be telling the truth." Because if he was, then maybe the rest wasn't as bad as she thought. And that probably made her an even bigger moron than she'd already proved herself to be.

When she got off the elevator, there was a reception desk directly in front of her. As Bryony walked up, the receptionist smiled. "Do you have an appointment?"

An appointment? It took her a moment to collect herself and then she nodded. "Rafael is expecting me."

Her voice sounded too husky and too unsure, but the receptionist didn't seem to notice.

"Are you Miss Morgan?"

Bryony nodded.

"Right this way. Mr. de Luca asked that you be shown right in. Would you like some tea or coffee?" With a glance down at Bryony's belly, she added, "We have decaf if you prefer."

Bryony smiled. "Thank you, but I'm fine."

The receptionist opened a door, and Rafael looked up from his desk. "Mr. de Luca, Miss Morgan is here."

Rafael rose and strode forward. "Thank you, Tamara."

"Is there anything you'd like me to get for you?" Tamara inquired politely.

Rafael shook his head. "See that I'm not disturbed."

Tamara nodded and retreated, closing the door behind her.

Bryony stared at Rafael, such a short distance away. She could smell him he was so close. She was at a complete loss as to how to act around him now. She could no longer maintain the outraged, jilted-lover act because if he couldn't remember her, he couldn't very well be blamed for acting as though she didn't exist for the past months.

But neither could she just take up where they'd left off and throw herself into his arms.

The result was tension so thick and awkward that it made her want to fidget out of her shoes.

He stared at her. She stared at him. One would never guess that they'd made a child together.

Rafael sighed. "Before this goes any further, there is something I have to do."

Her brows came together and then lifted when he took a step toward her.

"What?" she asked.

He cupped her face and stepped forward again until their bodies were aligned and his heat—and scent—enveloped her.

"I have to kiss you."

Four

Bryony took a wary step back but Rafael was determined that she wouldn't escape him. He caught her shoulders and pulled her almost roughly against him, swallowing up her light gasp just before his lips found hers in a heated rush.

He wasn't entirely certain what he'd expected to happen. Fireworks? His memory miraculously restored? Images of those missing weeks to flash into his head like a slide show?

None of that happened, but what did shocked the hell out of him.

His body roared to life. Every muscle tensed in instant awareness. Desire and lust coiled tight in his belly and he became achingly hard.

And hell, but she was responsive. After her initial resistance, she melted into his chest and returned his kiss with equal fervor. She wrapped her arms around his neck and clung to him tightly, her lush curves molded perfectly to his body. A body that was screaming for him to pin her to the desk and slake his lust.

He pulled back as awareness returned. For the love of God, what was he thinking? She was pregnant with his child, he couldn't remember her and yet he was ready to tear both of their clothes off and damn the consequences.

Well, at least she couldn't get pregnant again....

He ran a hand through his hair and turned away, his heart thudding out of control and his breaths blowing in ragged spurts from his nose.

Not his type? He shook his head. He'd never met a woman in his life with whom he shared such combustible chemistry.

When he turned back around, Bryony stood there looking dazed, her lips swollen and her eyes soft and fuzzy. It was all he could do not to haul her back into his arms to finish what he'd started.

"I'm sorry," he began before breaking off. "I just had to know."

Her eyes sharpened and the haze lifted away. "Know what?"

She crossed her arms over her chest and tapped her foot in agitation as she stared him down.

"If I could remember anything," he muttered.

Her lip curled into a snarl, baring her teeth. He was reminded of a pissed-off cat, and remembering that she'd decked him the night before, he took a step back.

"And?"

He shook his head. "Nothing."

She threw him a disgusted look and then turned to stalk out of his office.

"Wait a damn minute," he called as he started after her.

She made it to the door before he caught her arm and turned her around to face him.

"What the hell is your problem?"

She gaped at him. "My problem? Gee, I don't know. Maybe I don't appreciate being mauled as some sort of experiment. I get that this is difficult for you, Rafael, but you aren't the only one suffering here. You don't have to be such an ass."

"But—"

Before he could protest, she was gone again,

and he watched her walk away. At least she was wearing sensible shoes she wouldn't trip in.

He stood there arguing with himself over whether to go after her, but what would he say when he caught up? He wasn't sorry he kissed her even if it hadn't been a magic cure-all. It had told him one important thing. He couldn't get close to her without erupting into flames, which meant the likelihood of her carrying his child...?

Pretty damn good.

He strode back to his desk and picked up the phone. A few seconds later, Ramon answered with a curt affirmative.

"Miss Morgan has just left my office. See that she gets back to her hotel safely."

Bryony got off the elevator and exited the office building, no longer caring whether she and Rafael had dinner plans. Her jaw ached from the tight set of her teeth and tears stung the corners of her eyes.

She'd hoped for any sign of the Rafael de Luca she'd fallen in love with. Maybe she had also hoped that their kiss would spark...something. Or that maybe he would embrace the possibility that he'd felt something for her...once.

But there had been no recognition in his eyes when he'd pulled away. Just lust. Lust that any man could feel. A man could have sex with any number of women, but it didn't mean he harbored any deeper feelings for her.

The crisp air ruffled her hair and she started down the sidewalk, no clear direction in mind. It seemed colder than before and she shivered as she walked. Around her, horns honked, people jostled as they passed, dusk was settling and streetlights had started to blink on.

There was still plenty of light for her to walk the few blocks back to her hotel and she needed to let off some steam. She was flushed from Rafe's kiss and she was furious that he'd been so cold and calculating about it.

She'd felt like…a plaything. Like she hadn't mattered. Like she was just a set of boobs for his amusement.

But then that's likely all she'd ever been from the start.

She couldn't afford to be stupid a second time. Not until she had his guarantee—his *written* guarantee—that he wouldn't develop the land would she allow herself to think that his intentions toward her had been sincere.

She hugged her arms to her chest and stopped at a pedestrian crossing. A man knocked into her and she turned with a startled "Hey!"

He mumbled an apology about the time the light turned and the crowd surged forward. With her attention diverted she didn't feel the tug at her other arm until it was too late.

Her purse strap fell and her arm was nearly yanked from its socket as the thief started to run.

Anger rocketed through her veins and, reacting on instinct, she grabbed ahold of the strap with her other hand and tugged back.

The man was close to her own unimpressive height and nearly as slight, but grim determination was etched into his grimy face. He slammed into her, sending her sprawling to the pavement. She hit with enough impact to jar her teeth, but the strap was wrapped around her wrist now.

He jerked again and this time dragged her a few feet before he let out a snarl of rage and backhanded her. Her grip loosened and out of the corner of her eye she saw a flash of silver.

Fear paralyzed her when she saw the knife coming toward her. But her attacker slashed at the strap, sending her flying backward as the tension was released. He was gone, melting into

the crowd as she lay sprawled on the curb holding her eye.

It had only taken a few seconds. Under a
minute, surely. She heard someone shout and
then someone knelt next to her.

"Are you okay, lady?"

She turned, not recognizing the person who'd
spoken, and she was too stunned to respond.
Then she saw a sleek black car screech to a halt
in front of her and a huge mountain of a man
rushed out to hover protectively over her.

He moved with a grace that belied his enor-
mous size and he knelt in front of her, his hand
cupping her chin as he turned her this way and
that to examine her eye.

He barked rapidly into his Bluetooth but she
was too muddled to know what he said or to
whom he had spoken. She hoped it was the police.

"Miss Morgan, are you all right?" he asked
urgently.

"H-how do you know my name?"

"Mr. de Luca sent me."

"How would he know what happened?" she
asked in a baffled tone.

"He wanted to make sure you made it to your
hotel safely. I didn't catch you in time to give you

a ride. I was looking for you when I saw what happened."

"Oh."

"Can you stand?" he asked.

She slowly nodded. She'd certainly try. As he gently helped her to her feet, she clutched at her belly, worried that her fall had hurt her child.

"Are you in pain?" the man demanded.

"I don't know," she said shakily. "Maybe. I'm just scared. The fall…"

"I'm taking you to the hospital at once. Mr. de Luca will meet us there."

She didn't protest when he ushered her into the backseat of the car. He got in beside her and issued a swift order for the driver to take off. They were away and into traffic in a matter of moments.

She sank back into the seat, her hands shaking so badly that she clenched them together in her lap to try and quell the movement.

The giant beside her took up most of the backseat. He leaned forward and rummaged in an ice bucket in the console and a moment later held an ice pack to her eye.

She winced and started to pull away, but he persisted and held it gently to her face.

"Are you feeling any pain anywhere else?" he queried.

"I don't think so. I'm just shaken up."

His expression was grim as he pulled away the ice pack to examine her eye.

"You're going to have one heck of a bruise. I think it's a good idea to have a doctor check you out so you can be sure the baby wasn't harmed."

She nodded and grimaced when he put the ice pack back into place.

"Thank you," she murmured. "For your help. Your timing was excellent."

His face twisted with anger. "No, it wasn't. If I had been there a moment earlier, he wouldn't have hurt you."

"Still, thanks. He had a knife."

She swallowed the knot of panic in her throat and drew in steadying breaths. She could still see the flash of the blade as it slashed out at her. A shiver stole up her spine and attacked her shoulders until she trembled with almost violent force.

"I don't even know your name," she said faintly.

He looked at her with worried eyes as if he thought his name was the last thing that should be on her mind.

"Ramon. I'm Mr. de Luca's head of security."

"I'm Bryony," she said, before realizing he already knew her name. He'd called her Miss Morgan earlier.

"We're almost there, Bryony," he said in a steady, reassuring voice.

Was she about to melt down on him? Was that why he was staring at her with such concern and speaking to her as if he was trying to talk her down from the ledge?

She leaned her head back against the seat and closed her eyes. He followed with the ice pack and soon it was smushed up against her face again.

A few seconds later, the car ground to a halt and the door immediately opened. She opened her eyes as Ramon removed the ice pack and hurriedly got out of the car. He reached back to help her out and they were met by an E.R. tech pushing a wheelchair.

Astonished by the quickness in which they got her back to an exam room, she stared with an open mouth as she was laid on one of the beds by two nurses and they immediately began an assessment of her condition.

Ramon hung by her bedside, watching the medical staff's every move. As if sensing Bryony's bewilderment, Ramon leaned down and murmured, "Mr. de Luca is a frequent contributor to this hospital. He called ahead to let them know you'd be arriving."

Well, that certainly made more sense.

"The on-call obstetrician will be in to see you shortly," one of the nurses said. "He'll want to make sure all is well with the baby."

Bryony nodded and murmured her thanks.

The nurse went over a series of questions as she did her assessment. Bryony was a little embarrassed over all the fuss. Near as she could tell, all she'd suffered was a black eye and a bruised behind. But she wouldn't turn down the opportunity to make sure all was well with her baby.

She'd leaned back to close her eyes when the door flew open and Rafael strode in, his expression dark and his gaze immediately seeking out Bryony.

He hurried to her bedside and took her hand in his. "Are you all right?" he demanded. "Are you hurt? Are you in any pain?" He took a breath and dragged a hand through his hair in agitation. "The...baby?"

Before she could respond, his gaze settled on her face and his eyes darkened with fury. He tentatively touched her cheek and then he turned to Ramon, his jaw clenched.

"What happened?"

"I'm fine," Bryony said in answer to the barrage of questions. But Rafael was no longer concentrating his efforts on her. He was interrogating his head of security.

"Rafael."

When he still didn't stop his tirade of questions, she tugged at his hand until finally he turned back to her.

"I'm okay. Really. Ramon showed up just in time. He took good care of me."

"I should not have let you leave my office," Rafael gritted out. "You were upset and in no condition to be out on the streets. I'd thought Ramon would give you a ride home."

She shrugged. "I walked. He didn't catch up with me until after…."

Rafael looked hastily around and then dragged a chair to her bedside. He perched on the edge and stared intently at her.

"Has the doctor been in yet? What has he said about the baby? Are you hurt anywhere else? Did the bastard hit you?"

She shook her head at the flurry of questions

and blinked at the fierceness in his voice and expression. This wasn't a side of Rafael she'd ever seen before.

"The nurse said the on-call obstetrician would be in to see me shortly and that he would conduct an assessment to make sure all was well with the baby. And no, I'm not hurt anywhere else."

She raised her hand to her eye and winced when she pushed in on the already swelling area.

Rafael captured her hand and pulled it away from her eye.

"It's unacceptable for you to be walking the streets of New York City alone. I don't even like you staying in that hotel alone."

She smiled in amusement. "But it's your hotel, Rafael. Are you suggesting it isn't safe?"

"I'd prefer you were with me, where I know you are safe," he said through gritted teeth.

Her brows came together as she studied him. "What are you saying?"

"Look, we were going to be leaving together for Moon Island in a few days anyway. It's only reasonable that you'd stay with me until we depart. It will give us additional time to…reacquaint ourselves with one another."

She stared hard into his eyes, looking for… She

wasn't sure what she was looking for. What she saw, however, was burning determination and outrage that she'd been harmed.

He may not remember her, but his protective instincts had been riled, and whether he fully accepted that she carried his child, he was certainly concerned about both mother and baby.

Wasn't that a start?

"All right," she said softly. "I'll stay with you until we leave for the island."

Five

Rafael would have carried her into his penthouse if she'd allowed it. As it was he argued fiercely until she rolled her eyes and informed him that she was perfectly okay and that no one got carried around because of a black eye.

The reminder of her black eye just infuriated Rafael all the more. She was a tiny woman and the idea that some street thug had manhandled her—a pregnant woman—made his jaw clench. Even though the doctor had assured him that all was well with her pregnancy.

He wasn't sure what to do with himself. He was in new territory for sure. Bryony was the first woman he'd ever brought up to his penthouse and it felt as though his territory had been invaded.

"Would you like me to order in dinner?" he asked when he'd settled her on the couch. Surely it wasn't a good idea for her to go out and it was late.

"I'd like that, thanks," she said as she leaned her head back against the sofa.

He frowned when he saw the fatigue etched on her face. "You must be tired."

Her lips twisted ruefully and she nodded. "It's been an eventful couple of days."

Guilt crept up his nape until he was compelled to rub the back of his neck. He hadn't made things easier for her. She'd traveled a long way and then… Then things had gone all to hell.

He stood, irritated with himself. Why should he feel guilty about anything? He couldn't remember. God knew he'd tried. He went to bed frustrated every single night, hoping when he woke the next morning that everything would be restored and he could stop wondering about the holes. Stop wondering if he'd done something ridiculous like seduce and fall in love with a woman in the space of a few weeks.

It sounded so incredible that he couldn't wrap his head around it.

No, he shouldn't feel guilty. None of this had been his fault.

Except for the fact that he'd upset her and caused her to flee his office and she'd wound up being mugged as a result.

He studied her from across the room as he picked up the phone to call in their food order. She already looked as if she was asleep and he battled with whether to even bother waking her for dinner.

His gaze drifted to her belly and he swiftly decided against allowing her to sleep through the meal. It had likely been hours since she'd eaten anything.

He returned to her a moment later and settled on the chair next to the couch where she lay sprawled. "Would you like something to drink while we wait for the food?"

She stirred and regarded him lazily through half-lidded eyes. "Do you have juice? I feel a little light-headed."

He bolted to his feet. "Why didn't you say anything before now?"

She shrugged. "Quite frankly all I wanted was

a comfortable place to sit and relax. Having all those people around me was making me crazy."

He strode to the kitchen and rummaged in the fridge for orange juice. After checking the date on the carton, he poured a glass and went back into the living room.

This time he sat on the couch next to her and handed her the glass. She drank thirstily until half the contents were gone and then handed him back the glass.

"Thanks. That should do the trick."

"Is this something that happens regularly or is it just the excitement of the day?" he asked suspiciously.

"I'm borderline hypoglycemic. My blood sugar gets too low every once in a while. Pregnancy sort of messes with that and I have to be careful to eat regularly or I risk passing out."

Rafael swore under his breath. "What if you were to pass out when you were alone?"

"Well, the point is to make sure I don't pass out."

He scowled and then checked his watch. Only five minutes had passed since he'd placed the order.

"I'll be fine, Rafe," she said softly. "My grandmother is a diabetic. I'm well acquainted with how to handle low or elevated blood sugar."

The shortened version of his name, only used by his closest friends, slipped from her lips as if she'd used it a thousand times before. Coming from her, it sounded…right. As if he'd heard it before or maybe even encouraged her to use it.

He put a hand to his nape and looked away. Why couldn't he remember? If he had truly been involved with this woman, and if, like she'd said, they'd formed some romantic attachment—he couldn't quite bring himself to say *love*—then why would he shove her as far from his memory as he could?

She kicked off her shoes and then curled her feet underneath her on the couch before grabbing one of the cushions to snuggle into. It occurred to him that if they were a real couple he would have sat beside her and…cuddled. Or maybe offered her a foot rub. Weren't pregnant women supposed to have swollen ankles or something?

Which further proved to him that the idea of him falling in love and spending four weeks wrapped up in one woman was just…ludicrous. He dated. He even had relationships, but they were on his terms, which meant that his female companions didn't come to his penthouse. If they had sleepovers, it was done in one of his hotels. He certainly didn't engage in cuddling or cutesy things that a man would do for the woman he loved.

But then she glanced up and their eyes met. There was something in her gaze that peeled back his skin and squeezed his chest in a manner he wasn't familiar with. She looked…tired and vulnerable. She looked as if she needed…comfort.

Hell.

"Rafe, he got away with my purse," she said quietly.

He nodded. The police had come to the hospital to take her statement but it was doubtful they'd find her attacker.

"I didn't think…I mean everything happened so fast, and then at the hospital…" She lifted her hand in a helpless gesture that only made his desire to comfort her stronger.

"What is worrying you, Bryony?"

"I need to cancel my credit cards. My bankcard. God, he's probably already emptied all my accounts. My driver's license was in it. How am I supposed to get back home? I can't fly without identification."

The more she spoke, the more agitated she became. He slid onto the couch beside her and awkwardly put his arms around her.

"There's no need to panic. Do you have the telephone numbers you need?"

She shook her head and then laid it on his shoulder, her hair brushing across his nose.

"I can look them up on the internet if you have a computer."

He snorted. "Do I have a computer... I'm never without an internet connection of any kind."

She lifted her head and stared into his eyes. "You were when you were on the island."

His brow crinkled. "That's impossible. I wouldn't have just dropped off the map like that. I have a business to run."

"Oh, you kept in touch," she said. "But you often made your calls or answered emails in the morning or late at night. During the day you left your BlackBerry at my house while we explored the island."

He sighed. "See this is why I have such a hard time with the story you tell. I would never do something like that. It isn't me."

Her lips turned down in a frown and she leaned away from him.

To cover the sudden awkwardness, he stood and went to his briefcase to pull out his laptop. He stood for a long moment with his back to her just so he could compose himself and keep from turning and apologizing. He didn't want to hurt her, damn it. But one of them was crazy, and he didn't want it to be him.

He finally went back to the couch, opened the laptop and set it on a cushion next to her.

"If you have any problems canceling your cards or ordering new ones, let me know. I've typed up my address so you can have them overnighted here."

"And my license?" she asked in a tight, frustrated voice. "How am I going to get home?" She dragged her fingers through her hair, which only drew attention to the dark bruise marring her creamy skin.

"I'll get you home, Bryony. I don't want you to worry. Can you call your grandmother to fax a copy of your birth certificate? It's my understanding you can fly with the birth certificate but you'll be subjected to closer scrutiny by security."

"Couldn't we take your jet? Oh, I guess... Sorry." She broke off, seemingly embarrassed at her slip.

"I have more than one," he said dryly.

She continued to stare at him. "Then why aren't we taking it? Wouldn't it be easier to fly without identification if we were on a private jet?"

He cleared his throat and then rubbed the back of his neck. "Let's just say I have a newly developed phobia of flying on small planes."

She frowned. "I must sound so insensitive. I'm just... This has been a rotten trip all the way around."

"Yes, I suppose it has been for you," he murmured.

He eased back onto the couch beside her as she tapped intently on the keys. He hated how unsure of himself he was around her. But it was himself he was angry at. Not her.

If she was to be believed, her life had been completely upended. By him.

More and more he had an uneasy feeling that she was telling the truth. No matter how bizarre and unlikely such a scenario seemed. And if she was telling the truth, then he had to figure out what the hell he was going to do with the woman he supposedly loved and the child she carried. His child.

Six

"This reminds me of the nights we spent at my house," Bryony said as she forked another bite of the seafood into her mouth.

He paused, fork halfway to his own mouth, resigned to hearing more about his uncharacteristic behavior. But she said nothing and resumed eating, her gaze downcast, almost as if she knew how ill at ease he was.

But his curiosity was also piqued because, damn it, *something* had happened between them and she was the only key he had to recover the missing pieces of his memory.

He forced himself to sound only mildly inquisitive. "What did we do?"

A faraway look entered her eyes and she stared toward the window at the night sky. "We used to sit cross-legged on the deck and eat the dinner I'd cooked. Then I'd lay my head in your lap and you'd stroke my hair while we listened to the ocean and watched the stars."

Her voice lowered, catching on a husky note. "Then we'd go inside and make love. Sometimes we didn't make it to the bedroom. Sometimes we did."

The dreamy quality of her voice affected him fiercely. His body ached and he hardened at the images she provoked. It was suddenly very easy for him to see her spread out before him, his mouth on her skin, her fingers clinging to him as he brought them both pleasure.

He shook his head when he realized he was staring and that he was so tense that his muscles had locked. Part of him wanted to just get it over with. Take her to bed, have sex with her until they both forgot their names. His body was eager enough, but his mind was calling him a damn fool.

And she'd likely think it was some damn experiment after he'd basically admitted earlier that his kiss had been nothing more than that.

An experiment.

He wanted to laugh. Could he call desire so keen that his eyes had crossed when he'd looked at her an experiment?

Whether he wanted to admit it or not, they had compelling—uncontrollable—chemistry. Maybe he'd gotten so wrapped up in her that he'd lost all common sense. Maybe he'd made her rash promises in the heat of the moment. If her outrage was anything to go on, he at least hadn't been stupid enough to sign anything.

He needed her cooperation. He needed this deal. He had too many investors committed. Money had exchanged hands. Construction was on a tight deadline, and the last thing he needed was her making noises over him reneging on a deal.

She'd lifted her gaze and was now studying him so intently that he found her scrutiny uncomfortable. He studied her in return, finding himself mesmerized by her dark eyes. The delicate lines of her face called to him. He wanted to trace his fingers over her cheekbone and down to her jaw and then over the softness of her lips.

Had this been the way he'd felt when he'd first seen her? Logic told him it had to have been.

How could his reaction now have been any different than the first time he'd laid eyes on her?

"Why are you staring at me?" she asked in a low voice.

"Maybe I find you beautiful."

Her reaction wasn't what he expected. She lifted her nose in scorn and shook her head.

"I thought I wasn't your type."

"What I said was that you aren't my *normal* type."

Her lips twisted. "That isn't what you said. To quote you exactly, you said, 'You aren't my type.' That pretty much tells me you don't find me remotely appealing."

"I don't care what I said," he growled. "What I meant was that you aren't the type of woman I normally...date."

"Have sex with?" she asked mockingly. "Because we did, you know. We had lots and lots of sex. You were insatiable. In fact, unless you are the best damn actor in the world and can fake, not only an erection, but an orgasm as well, I'd say you're either lying now about me not being your type, or you're not terribly discerning when it comes to the women you sleep with."

He'd just been insulted but he was so distracted

by the sparks shooting from her eyes and how damn gorgeous she looked when she got sassy that he couldn't formulate a response.

"See, the problem is, a woman can get away with faking sexual attraction," she continued. "We can pretend all manner of things. Men? It's kind of hard to pretend attraction to a woman if your penis isn't cooperating."

"Holy hell," he muttered. "I think we've established that it's pretty damn obvious I'm sexually attracted to you. Whatever I may have thought in the past about my preferences in women obviously doesn't apply to you."

"So then you're willing to concede that you slept with me and that the child I'm carrying is yours?"

"Yes," he said through gritted teeth. "I'm willing to concede it's possible, but I'm not stupid enough to believe it's absolutely true until either I regain my memory, or we have DNA testing done."

Her top lip curled a moment and it looked as if she wanted to light into him again, but instead, she took a calming breath. "As long as you're willing to accept the possibility, I can work with that," she muttered.

"Were you always this…charming with me when we spent all this time together?"

She lifted one eyebrow. "What's that supposed to mean?"

"Just that I tend to like my women a little more…"

"Stupid?" she challenged.

He scowled.

"Weak? Mousy? Unchallenging?" she continued. "Or maybe you prefer them to simply nod and say 'yes, sir' to your every whim."

She broke off in disgust and regarded him as if he were some annoying bug she was about to squash.

He finally decided remaining silent was his best option so he didn't dig his hole any deeper.

She laid down her fork and raised her haunted gaze to his. He was surprised to see tears shimmering in her eyes, and his throat knotted. Damn. He hadn't wanted to upset her again. He wasn't *that* big of a jerk.

"Do you have any idea how hard this is for me?" she asked in a quiet, strained voice. "Do you know how difficult it is for me to see you again and not touch you or hug you or kiss you? I came here expecting to confront a man who scammed me in the worst possible way. I had resigned myself to it and there was nothing I wanted more than to wash my hands of you. But then you tell me this story about losing your memory and what am I supposed to do then? Now I have to consider that maybe you didn't lie to me, but I'm scared to death of believing that and then being wrong. Again. I have to put everything on hold until you regain your memory, and that sucks because I just don't know how to feel anymore."

He stared at her, frozen, an uncomfortable sensation coiling in his chest.

"I can't exactly walk away. It's what I accused you of and there's a part of me that thinks, 'What if he's telling the truth? What if he regains his memory tomorrow and remembers he loves you? What if it's all some horrible misunderstanding and we have a chance to get back what we had on the island?'"

She shoved her plate away and looked down as she visibly tried to collect herself.

"But what if I was right?" she whispered. "What if me sticking around hoping makes me an even bigger fool than falling for your lies to begin with? I have a child to consider now."

Before he could think twice about what he should say or do, he found himself reaching for her. It was impossible not to want to touch her, to offer her comfort. The pain in her expression was too real. Her eyes were clouded with moisture and hurt shimmered in their depths.

He pulled her into his arms and leaned back against the couch. For a moment she lay there stiffly, so still that he wondered if she held her breath.

He inhaled the scent of her hair and felt keen disappointment that it stirred nothing to life in his memories. Wasn't smell supposed to be the most powerful memory trigger?

Gradually she relaxed against him, her fingers curling into his chest as her cheek rested on his shoulder.

He dropped his mouth to the top of her head and stopped himself a moment before brushing his lips across her hair. It seemed the most natural thing to do and yet he knew tenderness wasn't a usual characteristic. It seemed too personal. Too intimate.

But the need to show her a more gentle side of himself was a physical ache.

"I'm sorry," he said truthfully. He had no love

for seeing this woman hurt. He didn't like to see anyone needlessly suffer. The fact that he was the source of her pain made him extremely uncomfortable.

"Just let me stay here a minute and pretend," she said. "Just don't say…anything."

He carefully laid his hand over her dark curls and did as she asked. He sat there, her head on his shoulder, one arm wrapped around her, his hand wrapped in her hair, and silence descended on them.

But the silence felt awkward to him, as if he should fill the gaps. Or ask questions. Something…

He glanced down at the soft curls splayed out over his chest. He could just feel the swell of her belly against his side.

Was this his reality? And if it was, why wasn't he running as hard as he could in the other direction?

It wasn't as if he was commitment-phobic. Okay, maybe a little, but it wasn't as if he'd endured some trauma in the past that made him leery of women. Nor was he some patsy who was afraid of allowing a woman to hurt him.

He hadn't ever committed because… Well,

he wasn't entirely certain. Men in relationships lacked a certain amount of control. They could no longer make solo decisions, and Rafael was used to making decisions in a split second—without conferring with someone else.

It wasn't a fluke that he owned his own business, not to mention had a partnership with three of his friends. His work took a lot of time. Time he wouldn't have if he had to worry about being home every night for dinner.

He liked being able to jet off at a moment's notice. He looked forward to business meetings—considered them a challenge. While he didn't have a lot of downtime, he did enjoy taking it at his leisure. He met Ryan, Devon and Cam at least once a year for golf, lots of alcohol and other pursuits only available to men who were not otherwise involved in a relationship.

Simply put, he'd never met a woman who made him want to give up all that. He damn sure couldn't imagine meeting her and giving up his life in a matter of four weeks. That kind of decision would have to be made over the course of years. Maybe never.

But on the other hand.

There was always a *but*.

As he stared down at the woman curled trust-ingly in his arms, something pulled at him. Some desire he hadn't ever acknowledged, one that would normally have horrified him—*should* hor-rify him.

He found himself wishing he could remember all the things she'd described to him, because all of a sudden, they sounded appealing.

And if that didn't scare the hell out of him, he wasn't sure what would.

Seven

"Rafael! Rafael! Wake up! Hurry!"

Rafael came awake with a start, his arms flying out as he pushed himself up from his bed. Bryony stood at his bedside, fully dressed, hopping around like her feet were on fire.

He threw his feet over the side and leaned forward. "What is it? Is it the baby? Are you hurt?"

She frowned a moment, shook her head and then grinned like a maniac. He rubbed his eyes and ran his hand through his hair.

"Then what the hell are you shouting about?" He glanced over at his bedside clock. "For God's sake, it's early!"

"It's snowing!"

She grabbed at his hand and started to pull. The covers fell away from his hips and they both went still. Her gaze dropped about the time his did and it was then he remembered he hadn't worn anything to bed, and worse, his penis was making its presence known in a not very subtle way.

He yanked the covers back over him as she stepped hastily back, pulling her sweater around her like a protective barrier. Hell, it wasn't as if he was bursting into *her* room trying to maul her.

"Sorry," she said. "I'll just go down by myself."

She turned and he scrambled out of bed, pulling the sheet with him.

"Wait a minute," he ordered. "What are you doing? Where are you going?"

Her eyes came alive again, brimming with excitement. The sparkle was infectious.

"Outside, of course! It's snowing!"

He glanced toward his window but he was too bleary-eyed to make sense of the weather. "Haven't you ever seen snow before?"

She shook her head.

"Are you serious?"

She nodded this time. "I live on an island off

the Texas coast. We don't exactly get snow there, you know."

"But you've been off the island. Haven't you ever been anywhere it snowed before?"

She shrugged. "I don't leave much. Mamaw needs me. I go to Galveston to do our shopping, but I do a lot of it online."

He saw her cast sidelong glances at the window as if she were afraid the snow would disappear at any moment. Then he sighed. "Give me five minutes to get dressed and I'll go down with you."

Her smile lit up the entire room and he was left with the feeling that someone had just punched him in the stomach. She nearly danced from his bedroom and shut the door behind her.

Slowly he dropped the sheet to the floor and stared down at his groin. "Traitor," he muttered.

He went into the bathroom, splashed water on his face and surveyed his unshaven jaw with a grimace. He never left his apartment without looking his best. There wasn't time for even a shower. The lunatic was probably already outside dancing in the snow.

He brushed his teeth and then went to his closet to pull out a pair of slacks and a sweater. He realized that since she'd never seen snow, she'd hardly be dressed for it, so he pulled a scarf and a cap from the top shelf.

Any of his jackets or coats would swallow her whole so he'd simply have to limit her snow gazing to a short period of time.

After donning his overcoat, he walked out of his bedroom to find Bryony glued to the window in the living room. Big flakes spiraled downward and her smile was like a child's at Christmas.

"Here," he said gruffly. "If you're going to go out, you need warmer things."

She turned and stared at the scarf and cap he held out and then reached for them, but he waved her hand off and looped the scarf around her neck himself, pulling her closer.

"You probably don't even know how to put one on," he muttered.

After wrapping the scarf around her neck, he arranged the cap over her curls and stepped back. She looked...damn cute.

Before he could do something idiotic, he turned and gestured toward the door. "Your snow awaits."

Bryony walked into the small courtyard that adjoined the apartment building, surprised that it was empty. How could everyone just stay inside on such a beautiful day? As soon as one of the flakes landed on her nose, she turned her face up and laughed as more drifted onto her cheeks and clung to her lashes.

She held out her hands and turned in a circle. Oh, it was marvelous and so pretty. There was just a light dusting on the patio surface, but along the fence railing and the edges of the stone planters, there was enough accumulation for her to scoop into a ball.

She scraped her hands together until she had a sizeable amount of snow and then she turned to grin at Rafael. He regarded her warily and then held up his hand in warning.

"Don't even think…"

Before he could finish, she let fly and he barely had time to blink before the snowball exploded in his face.

"…about it," he finished as ice slid down his cheek.

He glared at her but she giggled and hastily formed another snowball.

"Oh, hell no," Rafael growled.

As she turned to hurl it in his direction, a snowball hit the side of her face and melting ice slid down her neck, eliciting a shiver.

"I see you couldn't resist," she said with a smirk.

"Resist what?"

"Playing. But who could resist snow?"

He scowled. "I wasn't playing. I was retaliating. Now come on. You've seen the snow. We should go back inside. It's cold out here."

"Well, duh. It *is* snowing," she said. "It's supposed to be cold."

Ignoring his look of exasperation, she hurled another snowball. He ducked and she ran for cover when she saw the gleam in his eyes. She hastily formed another snowball then peered around one of the hedges in time to get smacked by his. Right between the eyes.

"For someone who doesn't play in the snow, your snowball fighting is sure good," she muttered.

She waited until he went for more snow and she nailed him right in the ass. He spun around, wiping at his expensive slacks—but who wore slacks to play in the snow for Pete's sake?—and then lobbed another ball in her direction.

She easily dodged this one and nailed him with another on the shoulder.

"I hope you know this means war," he declared.

She rolled her eyes. "Yeah, yeah. I made you lose that stuffy attitude once. I'll do it again."

His eyes narrowed in confusion and she used his momentary inattention to plaster him in his face.

Wiping the slush from his eyes, he began to stalk toward her, determination twisting his lips.

"Uh-oh," she murmured and began backtracking.

There wasn't a whole lot of room for evasion in the small garden, and unless she wanted to run back inside, there wasn't anywhere to go. Since it was probably his plan to herd her back indoors, she decided to meet him head-on and weather whatever attack he had in mind.

She began scooping and pelting him with a furious barrage of snow. He swore as he twisted and ducked and then he made a sound of resignation and began scooping snow from the stone benches and hurling it back at her as fast as he could.

Unfortunately for her, his aim was a lot better

and after six direct hits in a row, she raised her hands and cried, "Uncle!"

"Now why don't I believe you?" he asked as he stared cautiously at her, his hand cocked back to blast her with another snowball.

She gave him her best smile of innocence and raised her empty hands, palms up. "You win. I'm freezing."

He dropped the snowball and then strode forward to grasp her shoulders. He swept that imperious gaze up and down her body, much like he'd done the first time they'd met. This time it didn't rankle, for she knew that beneath that boring, straight-laced hauteur lay a fun-loving man just aching to get out. She just had to free him. Again.

She sighed at the unfairness of it all. It was like some sick joke being played on her by fate. Karma maybe. Though she was sure she'd done nothing so hideous as to have the love of her life and father of her child regard her as a complete stranger.

She shivered and Rafael frowned. "We should go inside at once. You aren't dressed for the weather. Did you bring nothing at all to wear for colder weather?"

She shook her head ruefully.

"We'll need to go shopping then."

She shook her head again. "There isn't a point. We'll be leaving to go back to Moon Island and it's still quite warm there."

"And in the meantime you'll freeze," he said darkly.

She rolled her eyes.

"You at least need a coat. I'll send out for one. Do you have a preference? Fur? Leather?"

"Uh, just a coat. Nothing exotic."

He made a dismissive gesture with his hands as if deciding that consulting with her was pointless. "I'll have it arranged."

She shrugged. "Suit yourself." He always did.

"When the doorman told me you were out playing in the snow, I asked him if the real Rafael had been abducted by aliens."

Bryony and Rafael both swung around to see Devon Carter leaning against one of the light posts just outside the door leading back into the apartment building.

"Very funny," Rafael muttered. "What are you doing here?" He took Bryony's hand in his.

Devon raised one lazy brow. "Just checking

in on you and Bryony. I heard there was some excitement yesterday."

Bryony grimaced and automatically put her other hand to the bruise she'd forgotten about until now.

"As you can see, she's fine," Rafael said. "Now if you'll excuse us, we're going up so she can change into some warmer clothing."

"Actually I was checking on you," Devon said with a grin. "Bryony strikes me as someone who can take care of herself."

Bryony cleared her throat as the moment grew more awkward. Devon wasn't worried about her. He was worried about Rafael in her clutches. Her face warm with embarrassment, she extricated her hand from Rafael's grasp.

"I'll just go up and leave you to, uh, talk. Did you leave the door unlocked?" Or whatever it was they did in these kinds of apartments. Rafael fished in his pocket and then held out a card. "You'll need this for the elevator."

She tucked it into her hand and hurried toward the door after a small wave in Devon's direction.

The two men watched her go and then Rafael turned to his friend with a frown. "What was that all about?"

Devon shrugged. "Just checking in on you, like I said. You've had a lot to digest over the past couple of days. Wanted to see how you were holding up and whether you'd remembered anything."

Rafael grimaced and then shoved Devon toward the door. "Let's at least go inside. It's cold out here."

The two men stopped in the coffee shop off the main lobby and Rafael requested the table by the fire.

"Things are fine," Rafael said after they were seated. "I don't want you worrying, nor do I want you plotting with Ryan and Cam to protect me for my own good."

Devon sighed. "Even if I think this idea of yours to jet off to this island is a damn foolish idea?"

"Especially then."

Devon sipped at his coffee and didn't even attempt to sugarcoat his question. But then that wasn't Devon. He was blunt, if anything. Cut and dried. Practical to a fault.

"Are you sure this is what you want to do, Rafe? Do you really think it's a good idea to go off with this woman who claims to be pregnant with your child? It seems to me, the smarter thing to do would be to call your lawyer, have paternity testing done and sit tight until you get the results."

Rafael's lips were tight as he stared back at Devon. "And what then?"

Devon blinked. "Well, that depends on the outcome of the tests."

Rafael shook his head. "If it turns out that I'm the father, if everything she claims is true, then I will have effectively denied her for the entirety of the time I wait for the test results. If she's telling the truth, I've already dealt her far too much hurt as it is. How can I expect to mend a rift if I have my lawyer sit on her while we wait to see if I'm going to be a father?"

Devon blew out his breath. "It sounds to me like you've already made up your mind that she's telling the truth."

Rafael dragged a hand through his hair. "I don't know what the truth is. My head tells me that she couldn't possibly be telling the truth. That the idea of me falling head-over-ass for her in a matter of weeks is absurd. It sounds so ludicrous that I can't even wrap my head around it."

"But…?"

"But my gut is screaming that there is definitely

something between us," Rafael grimly admitted. "When I get near her, when I touch her… It's like I become someone else entirely. Someone I don't know. I hear the conviction in her voice when she talks of us making love by the ocean and I believe her. More than that I *want* to believe her."

Devon let out a whistle that sounded more like a crash-and-burn. "So you believe her then."

Rafael sucked in his breath. "My head tells me she's a liar."

"But your gut?"

Rafael sighed because he knew what Dev was getting at. Rafael always went with his gut. Even when logic argued otherwise. And he'd never been wrong.

"My gut tells me she's telling the truth."

<u>Eight</u>

"Do you feel well enough to travel?" Rafael asked Bryony over dinner.

Bryony looked up from the sumptuous steak she was devouring to see Rafael studying the bruise on her face.

"Rafael, I'm fine."

"Perhaps you should see an obstetrician before we leave the city."

"If it makes you feel any better, I'll go see my doctor as soon as we get to the island, but I'm certainly capable of traveling. Unless you have matters to attend to here? I can go ahead of you if you can't get away yet."

Rafael frowned and put down his fork. "We'll

go together. It's important we retrace all our steps and follow the same pattern we did when I was there before. Perhaps the familiarity will bring back my lost memories."

Bryony cut another piece of her steak, but paused after she speared it with her fork. "What does your doctor say?"

Rafael became visibly uncomfortable. Even though the table they'd been seated at provided complete privacy from the other patrons, he glanced around as if the idea of anyone overhearing his personal business caused him no end of grief.

His lips pursed in distaste and then he finally said, "He thinks there's a psychological reason behind my memory loss. If I was so happy and in love then why would I want to forget? It makes no sense."

She was unable to control the flinch. Her fingers went numb as she realized how tightly she gripped the fork.

"I didn't say that to hurt you," he said in a low voice. "There's just so much I don't understand. I want to go back because I want to find the person I lost while I was there. The man you say you loved and who loved you is a stranger to me."

"Apparently we're both strangers to you," she said quietly. "Maybe that man doesn't exist. Maybe I imagined him."

Rafael's gaze dropped down her body to where her belly was hidden by the table. "But neither of us imagined a child. He or she is all too real, the one real thing in this whole situation."

She couldn't keep the sadness from her expression. The corners of her mouth drooped and she shoved her plate aside, her appetite gone.

"Our baby isn't the only real thing in our relationship. My love for you was real. I held nothing back from you. I guess we won't know whether you were real when you were with me. You deny that you could be that person. You deny it with your every breath. And I'm supposed to forget all of this denial if you suddenly remember you did and do love me."

She dropped her hands into her lap and wound her fingers tightly together as she leaned forward.

"Tell me, Rafael, which man would I believe? The man who tells me I'm not his type and that he couldn't possibly have loved me, or the lover who spent every night in my arms while we were on the island? No matter what you remember tomorrow, or the next day, I'll always know that a part of you rebels at the mere thought of being with me."

She could tell her words struck a chord with him. Discomfort darkened his features and regret simmered in his eyes. He splayed his hand out in an almost helpless gesture.

"Bryony, I…"

She gave a short, forceful shake of her head. "Don't, Rafael. Don't make it worse by saying you didn't mean it. We both know you did. At least you've been honest. You just need to re-member that you're not the only victim in this."

"I'm sorry," he said, and she knew he meant it.

He reached across the table and slipped his hand over hers. For a moment he stroked his thumb across her knuckles and then he gently squeezed.

"I really am sorry. I'm being a selfish bastard. I know this has to hurt you and that none of this is easy for you. Forgive me."

Her heart squeezed at the sincerity in his eyes. It was all she could do not to throw herself into his arms and hold on for all she was worth. She wanted to whisper to him that she loved him. She wanted to beg him never to let her go. But all she could do was stare across the table in help-less frustration.

"What if you never remember?" she asked, voicing her greatest fear.

"I don't know," he said honestly. "I hope it doesn't come to that."

She leaned back in her seat, slipping her hand from underneath his. The heaviness in her chest was a physical ache, one that clogged her throat and made it hard to breathe.

"What have you packed?" she asked lightly, forcing a smile.

He looked confused by the abrupt shift in con-versation. "I haven't yet."

She raised an eyebrow. "We leave in the morn-ing and you don't know how long you'll be gone. Aren't you leaving it to the last minute?"

He grimaced. "I wasn't sure what to pack. You mentioned things like swimwear and flip-flops."

She laughed as some of the tension in her chest eased. "Well, it's too cold to swim. The weather is still quite warm but the water is chilly. But we can buy you shorts and flip-flops like we did before. We can't have you wearing suits all the time, and your expensive loafers will just get ruined."

"I'm trusting you," he muttered. "Since you swear I did this before."

"And it didn't kill you," she teased. "When I was done with your makeover, you looked more relaxed and less like a stuffed shirt."

"You're implying I'm stuffy?" he asked in mock outrage.

"Oh, you were. Totally stuffy."

"I don't want to stand out this time. I'd like to keep my…problem…as private as possible."

"Of course," Bryony murmured.

He sat back in his chair and fiddled with his wineglass, though he didn't pick it up to drink. He turned in the direction of the band playing soft, mellow jazz and then back to her, his expression thoughtful.

"Tell me, Bryony. Did we ever dance?"

Caught off guard by the question, she shook her head mutely.

He stood and held his hand out to her. "Then dance with me now."

Mesmerized by the husk in his tone, she slipped her hand into his and allowed him to pull her to her feet. He led her onto the dance floor and slid his palm over her back as he pulled her into his embrace.

She closed her eyes and sighed as she melted against him. His warmth wrapped tantalizingly around her and his scent brushed over her nose. She inhaled deeply, holding his essence in the deepest part of her.

Oh, how she'd missed him. Even when she'd hated him, when she'd thought the absolute worst, she'd lain awake at night remembering the nights in her bed when they'd made love with the music of the ocean filling the sky.

She was acutely aware of him as they swayed in time to the sultry tones. He cupped her to him possessively, as if telling the world she belonged to him. It was nice to get lost in the moment and her daydreams.

As he turned her, she tilted her neck and gazed up at him as he tucked her hand between them, his thumb caressing the pulse at her wrist.

"You are an interesting dilemma, Bryony."

She raised her brows. "Dilemma?"

"Conundrum. Puzzle. One of the many things I can't seem to figure out lately."

She cocked her head to the side in question.

"I swear I have no memory of you. I look at you and draw a blank. But when you get close to me, when I touch you…" His voice dropped to a mere whisper and it sent a shiver racing down her spine. "I feel as though…"

"As though what?" she whispered.

He had a slightly bewildered look on his face as if he were searching for just the right word. Then finally he sighed and stared down at her, his gaze stroking over her skin.

"We fit," he said simply. "I have no explanation for it, but it just feels…right."

Her heart sped up. Hope pulsed in her veins, the first real hope she'd had since hearing his fantastic story. She didn't know whether to squeeze him or kiss him, so she stood there as they swayed with the music and smiled so brilliantly that her cheeks hurt.

"Amazing that such a simple thing could make you so happy," he murmured.

"We do fit," she said, her voice catching as her throat throbbed with a growing ache. She reached up to frame his face and then she leaned up on tiptoe to brush her lips across his.

She meant it to be a small gesture of affection. Maybe a reminder of what they'd once shared. Or maybe to just reaffirm the sensation to him that they fit. But he didn't allow her to stop there.

Cupping his hand to the back of her head, he

wrapped his other arm around her waist and hauled her up until her lips were in line with his.

There was nothing tentative about his kiss. No hesitancy as he attempted to find his way back. It was as if they'd never been apart. He kissed her like he'd kissed her so many times before, only this time… There was something different she couldn't quite put her finger on. More depth. More emotion. It wasn't just sexy or passionate. It was…tender.

Like he was apologizing for all the hurt. For the separation and misunderstanding. For what he couldn't remember.

She sighed into his mouth, sadness and joy mixing and bubbling up in her heart until she was overwhelmed by it all. When he finally drew away, his eyes were dark, his body trembled against hers, and as he eased her down, his hand slid up her arms to cup her face.

"Part of me remembers you, Bryony. There's a part of me that feels like I've come home when I kiss you. That has to mean something."

She nodded, unable to speak as emotion clogged her throat. She swallowed several times and then finally found her voice.

"We'll find our way back, Rafe. I won't let you

go so easily. When I thought you didn't want me, that you'd played me, it was easy to say never again. But now that I know what happened, I won't give up without a fight. Somehow I'll make you remember. It's not just your happiness at stake. It's mine, too."

He smiled and stroked a thumb over one cheekbone. "So fierce. You fascinate me, Bryony. I'm beginning to see how it could be true that I was so transfixed by you from the start."

Then he leaned down and kissed her again, the room around them forgotten. "I want to remember. Help me remember."

"You'll get it back," she said fiercely. "We'll get it back. Together."

Nine

The flight back to Houston was much better than her trip to New York. On the way she'd been squeezed between two men who she swore had to be football players. She hadn't been able to move and had spent the entire time being miserable.

She and Rafael occupied the first two seats in first class, and once they'd taken off, she'd reclined without guilt, since there was plenty of room between the rows.

By the time they landed in Houston, she actually felt rested and ready for the drive from the airport.

Apparently Rafael had ideas of having a driver take them to the island.

"My car is here. There's no reason for us not to take it," she insisted as they stood in baggage claim.

"We would both be more comfortable if you let me see to the travel arrangements."

"And what am I supposed to do without my car? We'll need it on the island. It's small but everything isn't in walking distance."

As their luggage piled up, Rafael sighed. "All right. We'll take your car. But it's senseless for you to drive when we've already been traveling half the day."

She rolled her eyes and bit her lip to keep from making a remark about spoiled men.

She grabbed a cart for their luggage and Rafael piled it up and pushed it as she led him to the parking garage.

"Where is the damn parking lot?" he demanded. "In Galveston?"

"It's a bit of a walk," she admitted. "But it's all indoors and then we'll take the elevator to the top level."

"Why did you park on the roof?"

She shrugged. "I just kept going around and around and then suddenly I was on the roof. It's the same as parking anywhere else."

He shook his head as they trudged down the long corridor. When they finally got to the elevator, Bryony breathed in relief. A few moments later, they were on the roof and she took out her keys to remotely unlock the car.

"What the…"

She cast him a puzzled look.

"That's your car?" he asked.

She looked toward the MINI Cooper and nodded. "Is something wrong?"

"You expect to fit me *and* the luggage in this tin can?"

"Quit being so grumpy," she said mildly. "We'll manage. It does have a luggage rack. I'm sure I have a bungee cord in the trunk."

"Who the hell carries around bungee cords?"

She laughed. "You never know when they'll come in handy."

They filled the trunk and then piled suitcases into the back until the bags were stacked to the roof of the car.

"There," she said triumphantly as she shut the door. "We didn't even have to use the bungee cords."

"Unfortunately we didn't push the passenger

seat back before we stored all the luggage," he said dryly.

Bryony winced when she saw him fold his legs to get into the front seat. His knees were pushed up into the dash and he didn't look at all comfortable.

"Sorry," she mumbled as she got into the driver's seat. "I wasn't thinking. No one who ever rides in my car has such long legs."

"How do you plan to drive the baby around after he or she is born?"

Bryony reversed out of the parking space and then drove toward the exit. "In a car seat, of course."

"And where do you think the car seat will fit in here? Even if you crammed it in, if you got into a wreck, neither of you would likely survive. Someone could run right over you in this thing and probably not even realize it."

"It's what I have, Rafael. There's not a lot I can do about it. Now let's talk about something else."

"How far of a drive is it?"

She sighed. "An hour to Galveston from the airport. Then we take a ferry to Moon Island. It's about a half-hour ferry ride so we should be there in under two hours barring any traffic issues."

It was a bad thing to say. Thirty minutes later, they were completely stalled on I-45. Bryony cursed under her breath as Rafael fidgeted in his seat. Or at least tried to fidget. He couldn't move much and he looked as if he was ready to get out and walk. It would probably be faster since traffic hadn't moved so much as an inch in the past five minutes.

"I know what you're going to say," she said when she saw him turn toward her. "We should have left my car at the airport. Yeah, I know that now, but really, traffic jams are a fact of life in Houston."

A smile quirked at the corners of his mouth. "I was actually going to say it's a good thing I went to the bathroom before we left the airport."

She heaved a sigh. "Just be grateful you aren't pregnant."

He arched an eyebrow. "Want me to take over?"

She shook her head. "You'd never be able to drive with your knees jammed to your chin. Let's find something to talk about. Music would just irritate me right now."

He seemed to think for a moment and then he said, "Tell me what you do. I mean, do you work?

You said you took care of your grandmother but I wasn't sure if that was a full-time task or not."

Bryony smiled. "No. Mamaw is still quite self-sufficient. I wouldn't say I take care of her as much as we take care of each other. She's been sicker lately, though. As for what I do, I'm sort of a Jill of all trades. I do a little bit of everything. I'm the go-to gal on the island for whatever needs doing."

He looked curiously at her.

"Basically I'm a consultant if you want a posh name for my job. I'm consulted on all manner of things, though nothing you'd probably think was legitimate," she added with a laugh.

"You have me curious now. Just what exactly are some of the things you do?"

"One day a week I take care of the mayor's correspondence. He's an older gentleman, and he's not fond of computers. Or the internet for that matter. He likes old-school things like actual newspapers, print magazines, watching the news on the local channel instead of surfing to CNN. That sort of thing. He doesn't even have cable if you can believe it."

"And this guy got elected?"

Bryony laughed. "I think you'll find that our

island is pretty tolerant of being old-fashioned. It's a bit of a throwback. While you can certainly avail yourself of all the modern conveniences such as internet, cable TV and the like, a large percentage of our population is quite happy in their technology-challenged world."

Rafael shook his head. "I'm shuddering as you speak. How can anyone be happy living in the Dark Ages?"

"Oh, please. You enjoyed it well enough yourself once I finally weaned you off your Black-Berry and your laptop. You went a whole week without using either. A week!"

"Surely a record," he muttered.

"Oh, look, traffic is moving!"

She put the MINI Cooper into gear as cars began to crawl forward. She checked her watch to see that they'd already lost an hour; it would be close to dark by the time they arrived on the island.

Still, the delay couldn't dim her excitement. It was foolish of her to get her hopes up, but she wanted so badly to relive her time with Rafael on the island. Take him through all the steps they'd taken before.

She wanted him to remember. Because if he

didn't, things would never be the same for them. He'd resisted the idea of being with her. Her only hope was for him to remember and then…

Then just as she'd told him the night before, she'd forever have to live with the fact that at least some part of him recoiled at the idea of them being lovers.

"Penny for your thoughts?"

She grimaced as she navigated her way down the interstate. "They aren't worth that much."

"Then don't think them."

To her surprise, he leaned over, curled his hand around her nape and massaged lightly, threading his fingers through her thick hair. It was tempting to close her eyes and lean her head all the way back but then they'd have a wreck and never get off this damn interstate.

"I'm nervous, Rafael," she admitted.

She bit her lip, wondering if she shouldn't just shut up, but she'd always had this habit of being completely honest. It wasn't in her makeup to shy away from the bald truth, no matter how uncomfortable. She always figured if people talked more about their issues then there wouldn't *be* so many issues.

Rafael—the old Rafael—hadn't minded her

speaking her mind. They'd enjoyed long conversations and she'd always told him what was occupying her thoughts.

But now, she had a newfound reservation against being so forthright. She hated feeling so unsure of herself.

"Why are you nervous?" he asked softly.

"You. Me. Us. What if this doesn't work? I feel like this is my only chance and that if you don't remember, I've lost you."

"Regardless of whether I regain my memory, we still have a child to think about. I'm not going to disappear just because I can't remember the details of his conception."

"You sound like you've accepted that I'm carrying your child."

He shrugged. "I've embraced the very real possibility. Until I'm proven wrong, I choose to think of it as my child."

Her heart did a little squeeze in her chest. "Thank you for that. For now it's enough. Until we figure out everything else, it's enough that you accept our baby."

"And you."

She turned to glance quickly at him before returning her gaze to the highway.

He lowered his hand from her neck to cover her hand that rested on his leg. "There is definitely something between us. If I accept that we made a child together, surely I have to accept that we were lovers, that you meant something to me?"

"I hope I did," she said softly.

"Tell me, Bryony, do you still love me?"

There was a note of raw curiosity in his voice. Almost as if he wasn't sure how he wanted her to answer.

"That's unfair," she said in a low voice. "You can't expect me to lay everything out when there's a real possibility we'll never be what we once were to each other. You can't expect me to admit to loving a man who thinks of me as a complete stranger."

"Not a stranger," he corrected. "I've already admitted that it's obvious we were something to each other."

"Something. Not everything," she said painfully. "Don't ask me, Rafael. Not until you remember me. Ask me then."

He reached up to touch her cheek. "All right. I'll ask you then."

Ten

After what seemed an interminable time, Bryony drove her little car onto the ferry and was immediately sandwiched by vehicles twice the size of hers.

Rafael had serious reservations about her driving around with a newborn in something only a little larger than a Matchbox car.

To his surprise, she opened her door and started to climb out.

"Where are you going?"

She ducked down to look at him through the window and flashed a wide smile. "Come on. It's a beautiful sunset. We can watch it from the railing."

Her exuberance shouldn't have surprised him by now. He'd gotten a taste of it in bits and pieces, but now that they'd left the city, she seemed to be even more excited, as if she couldn't wait to go back….

There was no doubt that he wanted to regain his memory. Having a gaping hole in his mind wasn't at all acceptable to someone like him, who was used to control in every aspect of his life. Now he was dependent on someone else to guide him and it made him extremely uncomfortable.

But in addition to knowing what happened during those lost weeks, he found himself hoping. Hoping that Bryony was right even if it meant a drastic change for him. He wasn't at all sure he was ready for fatherhood and a relationship. Love. If Bryony was to be believed… Love. It baffled him and intrigued him all at the same time.

He didn't want to hurt her. At this point he'd do anything to keep from hurting her and so he hoped that some miracle had occurred on this island and that he'd be able to find that same miracle again.

He climbed out of the car and stretched his aching legs. He inhaled deeply, enjoying the tang of the salty air. A breeze ruffled his hair, but he noted it was a warm breeze despite the coolness of the evening. The air was heavier here but... cleaner, if that made sense.

Bryony, in her impatience—which he was fast learning was an overriding component of her personality—grabbed his hand and tugged him toward the rail where others had gathered. Some had chosen to remain inside their vehicles, but others, like he and Bryony were leaning over the side and staring at the burst of gold on the horizon. Pink-and-purple hues mixed with the strands of gold, and spread out their fingers until the entire sky looked as if it were alive and breathing fire.

"It's beautiful, isn't it?"

He glanced down at Bryony and nodded. "Yes, it is."

"You don't see too many sunsets," she said smugly.

"What's that supposed to mean?"

She shrugged. "You mentioned before when we used to sit out on my deck that it wasn't something you ever had time to do. You usually worked late and were always in too big a hurry. So I was determined to show you as many as I could while you were here. Looks like I get to do it all over again. Oh, look! Dolphins!"

He looked to where she was pointing to see several sleek, gray bodies arc out of the water and then disappear below the surface.

"They follow the ferry quite a bit," she said. "I look for them every time I make the trip to Galveston."

He found himself caught up in the moment and before he knew it, he was pointing as they resurfaced. "There they are again!"

She smiled and hooked her arm through his, hugging him close. It seemed the most natural thing in the world to extricate his arm and then wrap it around her. They stood watching as the dolphins raced through the water, with her tucked up close to his side.

He shook his head at the absurdity of it all. Here he was without his phone or an internet connection. He'd left his BlackBerry in the car. He was on a ferry, of all things, watching dolphins play as he held the mother of his child.

Much was said about near-death experiences and how they changed a person. But it would appear that he'd begun his great transformation act *before* his accident.

It was little wonder Ryan, Dev and Cam were so worried about him. They were probably back in the city researching mental hospitals in preparation for his breakdown.

He rubbed his hand up and down Bryony's arm and then pressed a kiss to the top of her head. Then he sighed. He had to admit, he was actually looking forward to being on the island and spending time with Bryony and not just because he was anxious to recover his memory.

She wrapped her arms around his waist and squeezed. Her hug warmed him all the way through but not in a particularly sexual way. It was comforting. It was like holding a ray of sunshine.

As strange as it might sound, he felt comfortable around her. A complete stranger. Someone, who before a few days ago, he hadn't remembered, and for all practical purposes had never laid eyes on.

Yeah, his statement the night before had been a little—okay, a *lot* corny—but it was absolutely true. They fit. She fit him. And he had absolutely no explanation for it, other than somehow, he'd lost his heart and soul on that island and then the entire event had been wiped from his mind.

Okay. He accepted it. Hell, he embraced it. He wasn't fighting it. He was ready for whatever lay ahead. So why couldn't he remember?

He held her tightly to him, his face buried in her fragrant, dark curls. Tentatively he slid his hand down to cup her belly, the first time he'd made an overt gesture to acknowledge the life inside her womb.

She stiffened momentarily and then slowly turned her face up so she could look at him.

He rubbed in a gentle back-and-forth motion, exploring the firmness of the swell. Something he could only define as magic tightened his chest and flooded his heart.

This was his child.

Somehow he knew it.

He was going to be a father.

The realization befuddled him and at the same time, he felt such a sense of awe. He hadn't planned on fatherhood. In fact, he'd always been extremely careful in his sexual relationships. Extremely careful. He'd bordered on phobic about an accidental pregnancy.

Had he purposely discarded protection with Bryony? Had he considered the fact that they could make a child? Had she entertained such a possibility?

He frowned as he remembered her outrage and anger that it hadn't been enough that he'd screwed her over, but that he'd made her pregnant, too. No, that didn't strike him as the reaction of a woman who'd embraced such a thing.

Evidently it hadn't been something either of them had planned, but it was also obvious he hadn't gone to great lengths to prevent it.

He kissed her upturned lips and she smiled as she snuggled closer to him. Then she sighed in regret and carefully pulled away.

"We're nearly there. We should go back to the car."

Bryony turned on her headlights as they rounded the sharp turn and began the drive north toward her cottage. She frowned when she saw several vehicles parked on the highway near her driveway.

Her heart began to pound as fear gripped her. Had something happened to Mamaw? She'd spoken to her grandmother just hours earlier when she and Rafael had landed in Houston. She'd sounded fine then and eager to see Bryony again.

She recognized one of the vehicles as belonging to Mayor Daniels. What would he be doing here?

She pulled into the gravel driveway and turned off the ignition. Her grandmother stepped out onto the front porch followed by Mayor Daniels, who wore a frown, and Sheriff Taylor, who didn't look any happier.

She opened her door and scrambled out. "Mamaw, is everything all right? Are you okay?"

"Oh, honey, I'm fine. Sorry if we worried you. The mayor and the sheriff had some questions." Her grandmother eyed Rafael as he got out of the passenger seat. "We all do."

Bryony frowned and looked over at Mayor Daniels. "It couldn't wait? We've been traveling all day and got stuck in a traffic jam on the interstate."

The mayor picked up his finger and began to shake it, as he did every time he was upset over something. The sheriff put a hand on his shoulder.

"Easy, Rupert, give her a chance to explain."

"Explain what?" Bryony demanded.

"Why a ferry full of construction equipment landed on our island yesterday and why they're set to start building some fancy new hotel on the land you sold to Tricorp Investment," the mayor said as he shook an accusing finger at Bryony.

She shook her head adamantly. "There must be some mistake, Mayor. I've been in New York City all week to straighten out this mess. Rafael would have told me if construction was already scheduled to begin. And I didn't sell to Tricorp. I sold to Rafael."

The sheriff grimaced. "There's no mistake, Bry. I questioned the men myself. Asked to see their permits. Everything is all legal. I even asked to see the plans. That whole stretch of the beach is going to be turned into a resort, complete with its own helicopter pad."

Her mouth dropped open and she turned to Rafael, dread and disappointment nearly choking her. "Rafael?"

Eleven

Rafael bit out a curse as he faced four accusing stares. Bryony's was confused, though, and a little dazed. Pain and bewilderment made their way across her face and the look in her eyes made him wince.

"Now see here," the mayor began as he stepped forward.

Rafael brought him up short with a jerk of his hand. He stared hard at the other man and the mayor took a hasty step back, nearly pulling the sheriff in front of him for protection.

"This is a matter between Bryony and myself," he said in an even voice. "As she said, we're tired. We've traveled all day, she's pregnant and she's dead on her feet. I won't stand here arguing with you in her driveway."

"But—" The mayor turned to the sheriff. "Silas? Are you going to let him get away with this?"

The sheriff sighed and adjusted his hat. "What he's doing isn't illegal, Rupert. It might be unethical, but it isn't illegal. He owns the land. He can do what he likes with it."

"Rafael? Did you approve this? Is it true they're starting construction?" Bryony asked in a strained voice.

Her grandmother stepped to her side and wrapped her arm around Bryony's waist. Her grandmother was a frail-looking woman and it irritated Rafael to no end that it was Bryony who looked the more fragile of the two at the moment.

"We'll discuss this in private," he said tightly.

"Do you want him here, Bry?" the sheriff asked.

Bryony raised a hand to her temple and rubbed as if she had no idea what to say to that question. Hurt crowded her eyes, and then deep fatigue, as if all her energy had been sapped in a single instant.

Knowing if he didn't take control of the situation, he'd likely be carted off to some second-rate jail cell, Rafael moved to Bryony's side and gently pried her away from her grandmother. He wrapped his arm around her waist and cupped his hand over her elbow.

"We'll talk inside," he murmured.

She stared up at him as if she searched for some shred of truth or maybe deceit. He couldn't be entirely sure what she was thinking.

Then she stiffened and looked toward the two men. "He's staying here, Silas. I appreciate your concern."

"And the construction?" Rupert asked in agitation. "What am I supposed to tell everyone? It wasn't me who sold the land to the outsider but it happened on my watch. I'll never win reelection if it becomes known that the island went to hell during my term."

"Rupert, shut up," Bryony's grandmother said sharply. "My granddaughter is upset enough without you yammering on about your political career."

"Come on, Rupert. Nothing good can come of us standing in her driveway at this hour. There'll be plenty of time to sort this out tomorrow," Silas said as he herded the older man toward his vehicle.

As he left, he tipped his hat to Bryony. "Let me know if you need anything, young lady."

Bryony gave him a tight smile and nodded her thanks. When the two men were gone, Bryony's grandmother hugged her.

"I'm glad you're home. I worry when you travel. Especially to a city like New York."

If Rafael had expected the older woman to turn on him in anger he was wrong. Instead she gently enfolded him in a hug and patted his cheek.

"Welcome back, young man. I'm glad you found your way back here."

With that, she walked down a narrow stone path in the grass that led to the adjoining yard.

"Will she be okay?" Rafael asked with a frown. "Should we take her home?"

Bryony sighed. "She lives next door. Just a few steps from my front door."

"Oh. Right. Sorry."

"Yeah, I know, you don't remember."

This time her tone lacked the patience and understanding she'd exhibited until now. There was an undercurrent of hurt that cut into him and pricked his conscience.

Hell. He'd once have argued that he didn't have a conscience when it came to business. Business was business. Nothing personal. Only now…it was definitely personal.

"Come on," she said. "We need to get all this luggage inside."

He put his hand on her arm. "You go in. I'll bring in the luggage. Don't argue. Go get something to drink or eat if you're hungry. I'll be in in just a moment."

She shrugged and walked to the steps leading onto the porch. A moment later, she disappeared into the house, leaving Rafael standing in the driveway staring at his surroundings with keen eyes.

So this is where he'd spent so many days and nights. This is where his life had supposedly undergone such a drastic change. He didn't feel anything other than that he was distinctly out of his comfort zone and in way over his head.

He carried the luggage in two trips to the front porch and then propped her door open and began lugging the bags into the living room.

As he stepped in, he stared around, absorbing the look and feel of the place Bryony called home. It reflected her personality to a T. Sunny, cheerful, a little cluttered, as if she were always in too much of a hurry to keep it spotless. It looked lived-in, nothing like his sterile apartment, which a cleaning lady made spotless every day regardless of whether he was in residence or not.

She stood with her back to him, staring out the French doors that led onto the deck. Her arms were wrapped protectively around her chest and when she turned, he could see the barricade she'd erected as surely as if it were a tangible shield.

"Did you know about the construction? Did you order it to begin?" she asked.

He sighed. "Do you want me to lie, Bryony? I won't. I've been nothing but truthful to you. Yes, I ordered construction to begin. I would have started much sooner but my accident delayed me significantly. My investors are anxious. They want to see progress in return for the money they've shelled out."

"You promised," she choked out.

He ran a hand through his hair and wished he could make this go away. At least until they had matters between them sorted out.

"You know I can't remember," he said. "As far as I knew, the land was bought, the deal closed, the property to do with as I liked. There was nothing in the contract that stipulated how I could use the land. I wouldn't have signed such a contract. The land is useless to me unless I develop it."

Damn it. Why couldn't he remember? Surely he wouldn't have made her such a promise. It defied all logic. Why on earth would he have bought the land and promised not to develop it?

He closed the distance between them and slid his hand over her shoulder. She flinched and lifted her shoulder away, but he kept his hand against her skin.

"Bryony, again, I'm not doing this to hurt you. I don't remember. You say I made you a promise, but I have no proof of that. What I do have is proof of sale. I have your signature on the closing documents as well as a copy of the bank draft issued to you from my bank."

She turned to face him again, her eyes red-rimmed. She looked to be fighting tears with every bit of her power.

"I made it clear from the start that I wouldn't sell to you unless you promised it wouldn't be developed on a large scale. Obviously I can't control what a new owner does with the land, but I'd hoped for something in keeping with the integrity of our community here. You looked me in the eye and you promised me that you had no such plans. That was a lie, Rafael. It's an obvious lie because clearly you had investors lined up, plans drawn, a schedule planned. You yourself just said that your accident delayed the groundbreaking significantly."

Rafael swore because one of them had to be lying and he didn't want it to be him. He didn't want it to be her.

"Damn it, Bryony, I refuse to feel guilt for something I can't remember."

"We should get some sleep," she said dully. "There's little point in arguing over this when we're both tired and I'm upset. I'll show you to the guest room. It has its own bathroom. There are towels and soap, everything you should need."

And just like that, she was dismissing him. She'd withdrawn and he was treated to the cold, angry woman she'd been the first night in New York when she'd confronted him at his event.

He drew in a breath, feeling like a fool for what he was about to say, but it rushed out before he could think better of it, before he could question his sanity.

"I'll put a temporary halt to construction. Tomorrow. I'll go to the site myself. Until we sort things out between us and I regain my memory, I'll halt the groundbreaking."

She blinked in surprise, her mouth forming a silent O. From all appearances it was the last thing she'd expected him to say, and he was suddenly glad of it. Fiercely glad that he'd caught her off guard.

"Really?"

He nodded. "I'd go tonight but no one will be at the site and I have no idea where they're staying, but if I'm there at dawn in the morning, I'll make sure nothing is done until I give the okay to begin."

Once again she surprised him by launching herself into his arms and hugging him so tight he struggled to breathe. For such a small woman, she possessed amazing strength.

"Every time I think you've let me down, you do something to completely change my mind," she whispered fiercely. "Every time I think I've lost the Rafael I fell in love with, you do something to make me realize he's still there and I just have to find him again."

He wasn't sure he liked the sound of that. As if he was some sort of Dr. Jekyll and Mr. Hyde.

Hell, maybe he *was* crazy. It was the only explanation behind the past few months of his life.

Most men bought a flashy sports car, had an affair or hooked up with a girl barely out of school in their midlife crisis. Apparently he did bizarre things like fall in love and throw away a multimillion-dollar deal.

Ryan, Dev and Cam were going to kill him.

Twelve

"You did *what?*"

Rafael held the phone away from his ear and winced at the string of expletives that flooded the airways.

"I'm coming down there. We all are," Devon said. "This is precisely what I was afraid of happening. You get down there and she has you by the balls. Make me the bad guy. I don't care, but construction has to begin immediately. We're already months behind schedule."

Rafael paced back and forth over the slight bluff overlooking the beach while Bryony waited in the car. The crew hadn't been happy that they were being asked to stand down, until Rafael informed them they'd be paid full wages during the temporary layoff. He'd stressed *temporary* and hoped like hell that he would have this resolved in a few days' time.

He didn't offer that little tidbit to Devon. Devon would really lose his composure if he knew Rafael was footing the bill for a crew of construction workers to sit around and enjoy beach life for the next few days.

"You stay your ass in New York," Rafael said. "I don't need you and Cam and Ryan to babysit me. It's the right thing to do, Devon. Until I know what the hell I promised or didn't promise or whatever else happened while I was down here the first time, the right thing to do is wait."

"Since when have you ever been concerned with doing the right thing?" Devon asked incredulously. "We're talking about the king of get-it-done, it's business, not personal, whatever it takes, score the deal. Are you getting soft in your old age or has she messed with your head so much that you no longer know up from down?"

Rafael scowled. "You make me sound like a complete bastard."

"Yeah, well, you are. Why should that bother

you now? It's what's made you so successful. Don't go growing a conscience on me now."

Rafael frowned even harder. "What do you know about this deal, Devon? What aren't you telling me?"

There was a long silence. And then his friend said, "Look, I don't know what happened down there. What I do know is that before you left New York, you said quite clearly that you'd come back with a signed bill of sale and you didn't give a damn what you had to do to achieve it."

"Son of a bitch," Rafael muttered. "That's not helping my case here."

"Why do you want it to help your case? You've got the land. You've got our investors on board. The only thing standing in our way right now is you."

Rafael stared back at the car to see that Bryony had gotten out and leaned against the door. Her hair blew in the morning breeze and it was a little chilly. She hadn't worn a sweater.

"Yeah, well, for now I'm not moving," he said quietly. "I'll accept full responsibility for this."

"Damn right you will," Devon said in disgust. "We've all made sacrifices, Rafael. We're on the verge of being huge. With this resort deal and the merger with Copeland hotels, we'll be the largest luxury resort business in the world. Don't screw it up for all of us."

Rafael sighed. Yeah, he knew they'd made sacrifices. Devon was even marrying Copeland's daughter to cement this deal. They were close to having everything they'd ever wanted. Success beyond their wildest imaginations.

And he'd never felt worse or more unsure of himself in his life.

"Trust me on this, Dev. Give me some time, okay? I'll make it right. I've never not come through before. But this is my future we're talking about here."

Rafael heard the weary sigh through the phone. "One week, Rafe. One week and if ground isn't broken, I'm coming down there and I'm bringing Ryan and Cam with me."

Rafael ended the call and shoved the phone into his pocket. One week. It seemed a ridiculous amount of time to decide the fate of his entire future. And Bryony's future. The future of his child.

He blew out his breath and walked away from the beach toward Bryony's car. She was probably tired. He'd bet that neither of them had slept much the night before. He'd seen dark circles under her eyes when they'd left her cottage before sunup to drive to the construction site.

With a week's reprieve, it was time to concentrate on the most important issue at hand—regaining his memory and figuring out his relationship with Bryony Morgan.

As Rafael strode back toward the car, Bryony regarded him warily. He looked angry and determined. Whatever phone call he'd made, it hadn't been pleasant. She could hear his raised voice all the way inside the car, though she couldn't make out what it was he said.

True to his word, he'd given the order to suspend groundbreaking. It hadn't taken long for her cell phone to start ringing. Rupert had been first, congratulating her on keeping Rafael de Luca in line. Bryony had rolled her eyes and bitten her tongue. As if anyone could leash Rafael de Luca. No, whatever reason he had for agreeing to postpone construction, it hadn't been because she'd asked him to.

Her pride had already taken enough of a beating. She wasn't going to beg him.

Then Silas had called to confirm that construction had indeed been halted and then expressed his concern that the workers were now on the island with nothing to do for the next however many days. He worried about the implications. As if Bryony had any experience with enforcing the law.

Still, she had to remember that a lot of people counted on her to keep things running smoothly. It was what she did. Never mind that her life was in shambles. She didn't offer any guarantees about keeping her own affairs straight.

When Rafael arrived, he didn't say anything. He took the keys from her and guided her around to the passenger side.

When he got in, she eyed him sideways. "Everything okay?"

"Fine."

He started the engine and drove over the bumpy dirt path back to the main road and then accelerated.

"Feel like some breakfast?"

It sounded like he grunted in return, but she couldn't be sure. Still, he hadn't said no, so she took it as an affirmative.

"I'll make your favorite."

He glanced sideways at her. "My favorite?"

"Eggs Benedict."

"Yeah, it is," he mumbled. "I guess I told you that before."

"Uh-huh."

Clearly he wasn't in a talkative mood. He looked downright surly. She was more of a morning person, but Mamaw wasn't, and she often told Bryony she was too cheerful for her own good before noon. Mamaw didn't have any compunction about telling her to shut up and go away, but Bryony guessed Rafael was too polite to do the same.

Funny, but she hadn't noticed him being particularly grumpy in the mornings before, but then more often than not, they'd slept late after a night of making love.

Just the memory of them waking in bed, wrapped around each other, had her cheeks warming and a tingle snaking through her body.

She missed those nights. And the mornings. Most of the time she'd cooked for them both, but at least twice, Rafael had risen while she still slept and brought her breakfast in bed.

So instead of saying anything further, she reached over and took his hand, squeezing it before lacing her fingers through his.

He looked surprised by the gesture, but he

didn't make any effort to extricate his hand from hers.

"Thank you."

He cocked his head.

"For doing that. It means a lot not just to me, but also to the people on this island."

He looked uncomfortable. "You need to understand that this is only a temporary solution. I can't suspend operations indefinitely. There are a lot of people counting on me. They've trusted me with their money. My partners are heavily invested with me. This is… This is huge for us."

"But you understand I would have never sold you the land if you hadn't given me your promise," she said. "The result would be the same. It's not as though I sold you the land under false pretenses."

Rafael sighed but then squeezed her hand. "For now let's not talk about it. There's no simple solution to all this whether I regain my memory or not."

For the first time she weighed his position in the matter. If all he'd said were true, then it couldn't have been easy for him to call off the operation.

Regardless of whether he'd lied to her before,

he'd done the honorable thing now and it was costing him dearly.

She leaned over and brushed her lips across his cheek. "I realize this isn't easy, but we all appreciate it. I've already gotten calls from the mayor and the sheriff. I'm sure there will be more before the day is out. You can expect to be courted by the locals while you're here. They'll want to present their case."

"Are they angry with you?" he asked. "The mayor didn't seem pleased with you last night. Do they all blame you?"

She blew out her breath. "They think I'm young and gullible. Some of them blame that and not me directly. They're too busy feeling sorry for me for being taken by a suave, debonair man. Others put the blame solely on my shoulders, as they should."

Rafael's face grew stormy. "It's your land. You can't allow others to guilt you into keeping it just because they don't want their way of life to change."

She shrugged. "I grew up here. They consider me a part of their family. Family doesn't turn their backs on each other. A lot of them think I did just that. Maybe I did. I knew that if you and

I were going to be together that I wouldn't stay here. I knew I'd have to make the move because your business is based in the city. At the time I didn't care."

He slowed to pull into her driveway and stopped the car. For a long moment he stared out the windshield before finally turning to face her.

"So you were willing to give up everything to be with me."

"Yes," she said simply. Throwing his words back at him, she continued. "I don't say that to hurt you. It's simply the truth and we've both been honest and blunt. I'm not trying to make you feel guilty."

"I don't know what to say."

She smiled. "Let's not say anything. Let's go eat instead. I'm starving. After breakfast we'll go buy you the things you need for your stay and then maybe we'll sit on the deck. Enjoy the day."

Strangely enough, it sounded blissful.

Suddenly, after a not-so-great start to the day, he found himself quite looking forward to the rest.

Thirteen

Bryony tugged Rafael from shop to shop in the town square where she made him try on more casual clothing. Jeans. Lord but the man looked divine in jeans. They cupped his behind in all the right places and molded to his muscular legs.

And a T-shirt. Such an unremarkable item of clothing but on him… A simple white T-shirt displayed his lean, taut body to perfection.

He looked uncomfortable when he came out of the dressing room. He had on the jeans and the shirt she'd picked out and he was barefooted. Barefooted.

She was standing there drooling over a barefooted man in jeans. And she wasn't the only one.

"Oh, my," Stella Jones breathed. "Honey, that is one fine specimen you've got there. He looks hot in the *GQ* stuff, don't get me wrong, but he fills out a pair of jeans like nobody's business."

Bryony shot the saleswoman a glare but had to admit she was right.

"Will this make you happy?" Rafael asked wryly as he turned, hands up.

"Oh, yeah," Bryony murmured. "Me and every other female on this island."

Stella chuckled. "Shall I bag up a few more pair like that one?"

"And T-shirts. Lots of T-shirts. I'm thinking white and maybe a red one."

"Green wouldn't be bad with those dark eyes and hair," Stella advised.

Rafael rolled his eyes. "I'm going back in to change while you ladies sort it out."

"No! No!" Bryony said in a rush. "Just let me pull off the stickers. No reason to change out of them. Stella will ring them up. You'll be more comfortable."

"And so will the rest of us," Stella said over her shoulder as she sashayed off to get the rest of the clothing.

Rafael grinned and sauntered toward Bryony. "So you like me in jeans?"

"I think *like* is perhaps too mild a word," Bryony muttered.

Although Bryony had been openly affectionate with Rafael the entire day, taking his hand, hugging him or twining her arm through his, he hadn't made any overt gestures of his own. But now he slid his arms around her and pulled her into his embrace.

He rested his hands loosely at the small of her back and then slid his fingers into her back pockets, pulling her closer until she was pressed against his chest.

"I like you in jeans, too," he said with a sly grin.

Her heart fluttered as she curled her arms around his shoulders.

"Yeah, but I'm wearing baggy jeans with an elastic maternity waist."

"They fit your behind just fine."

To emphasize his point he moved his fingers to where they were snug in her back pockets.

"We'll have the whole island talking," she murmured.

He snorted. "As if they aren't already? I think

everyone who lives here has been out to either look at us or tell me what a wonderful thing I did by stopping the construction. And I think it's a widely known fact that it's my child you're carrying. What else could they possibly talk about beyond that?"

"Okay, you have a point," she said wryly.

He leaned down and kissed her softly. "Why don't we take our jeans-clad selves back to your cottage and I'll fix us some lunch."

She raised her eyebrows. "What have you got in mind?"

"I don't know. It depends on what you have in your pantry. You cooked breakfast for us and you've taken me around town all morning. The least I can do is pamper you awhile. Are your feet tired?"

She laughed even as her heart squeezed at the concern in his voice.

"My feet are fine, but I wouldn't turn down a massage if you're offering."

He gave her a smile filled with genuine warmth. "I think that could be arranged."

She flung her arms around him and buried her face in his chest. "Oh, Rafael. Today has been perfect. Just perfect. Thank you."

When she pulled away, he had a befuddled expression on his face as if he didn't know quite how to respond to her outburst.

"I had no idea shopping for jeans made you so happy," he teased.

She flashed him a cheeky grin. "Only when I get to see you wear them."

He patted her affectionately on the behind and then gestured for her to go ahead of him. "Let's go then. All this shopping has worked up my appetite."

She laced her fingers with his, delighting in the sense of closeness that had quickly built between them. Whether he remembered or not, the moment they'd arrived, Bryony had sensed a change in Rafael. He'd reverted to the more relaxed, easygoing man with whom she'd fallen in love.

He may not see himself as someone who would get away from the stress of the business world, or someone who would leave his cell phone off or his computer put away for a period of days, but Moon Island had changed him. She'd like to think that his relationship with her had changed his priorities. Maybe it was fanciful and naive for her to think such things, but it didn't stop her

from hoping that he'd rediscover the island—
and her.

They drove back to the cottage but Bryony directed him to pull into her grandmother's driveway instead of her own.

"I want to check in with her and see how she's
doing. I've only talked to her on the phone for the
last week. I don't often leave her for long periods
of time."

Rafael nodded. "Of course. Would you prefer
I go ahead to your cottage and begin lunch?"

"Only if you want to. I don't mind if you come
unless you're uncomfortable. I'm only going to
talk to her a minute or two. Make sure everything's okay."

"Then I'll go with you," Rafael said. "I'd like to
get reacquainted. You two seem to be very close.
Did I spend a lot of time with her before?"

Bryony smiled. "You got along famously. You'd
drop in on her every other day or so whether I
was with you or not. You spoiled her by bringing
her favorite flowers and a box of goodies from
the bakery."

"I sounded…nice," he said, as though the idea
were ridiculous.

She paused in the act of opening her car door

and turned her head so she looked directly at him. "You say that as if you aren't…nice."

He shrugged. "*Bastard* has been used on more than one occasion to describe me. This morning being the most recent. I've been called a lot of things. Ruthless. Driven. Ambitious. Son of a bitch. You name it. But nice? I can't say that being thoughtful was ever a priority. It's not that I intended to be a jerk, but I was never really concerned about it."

"Well, you were wonderful to my grandmother and I loved you for it," she said. "You were wonderful to me, too. Maybe you don't associate with the right people."

He laughed at that. "Maybe you're right. I guess we'll see, won't we?"

Bryony's grandmother appeared on the front porch and waved for them to come in. Bryony reached over and squeezed Rafael's hand. "Stop worrying so much about what you were or weren't. No one says you have to stay the same forever. Maybe you were ready for a change. Here you could be whoever you wanted because no one knew you before. You got to have a fresh start."

He raised her hand and pressed a kiss to her

palm. "What I think is that you're a special woman, Bryony Morgan."

She smiled again and opened her car door. As she got out, she waved at her grandmother. "We're coming!"

Mamaw smiled and waved, then waited with the screen door open while Rafael and Bryony made their way up the steps.

"Good afternoon to you," Mamaw said cheerfully.

She pulled Bryony into a hug and then did the same with Rafael, who looked a little dumbstruck by the reception.

"Come in, come in, you two. I just sweetened a pitcher of tea and it's ready to pour. I'll get us some glasses. Have a seat on the back porch if you like. It's a beautiful day and the water is gorgeous."

Bryony tugged Rafael to the glass doors leading onto a deck that was similar in build to her own. The wood was older and more worn but it added character. The railings were dotted with potted plants and flowers. Colorful knickknacks and decorative garden figurines were scattered here and there, giving the deck an eclectic feel.

Bryony often thought it resembled a rummage

sale, but it so fit her grandmother's personality that it never failed to bring a smile to Bryony's face.

Mamaw didn't much believe in throwing things away. She wasn't a hoarder and she *would* part with stuff after a while, but she liked to collect items she said made her house more homey.

"It's beautiful out here," Rafael said. "It's so quiet and peaceful. There aren't many stretches of private beach like this. It must be amazing to have this all to yourself."

Bryony settled into one of the padded deck chairs and angled her head up to catch the full sun on her face. "It is," she said, her eyes closed. "The whole island is like this. It's why we're so resistant to the idea of commercially developing parts of it. Once the first bit of 'progress' creeps in, it's like a snowball. Soon the island would just be another tourist stop with cheesy T-shirts and cheap trinkets."

"What I purchased was just a drop in the bucket for an island this size. Surely you don't begrudge any development. You could have the best of both worlds. The majority of the island would remain unspoiled, a quiet oasis, while a very small section would be developed so that others could be exposed to your paradise."

She dropped her head back down, opening her eyes to look at him. "You sound just like a salesman. The truth is, the whole sharing-our-paradise-with-others spiel is precisely what we don't want to do. Call us selfish but there are numerous other islands that tourists can go to if they want sun and sand. We just want to be left alone. Many of the people who live here retired to this island precisely because it was private and unspoiled. Others have made their whole lives here and to change it now seems grossly unfair."

"Having one resort wouldn't ruin the integrity of the island and it would boost the economy and bring in an influx of cash from those tourists you all despise."

She smiled patiently, unwilling to become angry and frustrated and ruin a perfect day. Besides, biting his head off didn't serve her purpose.

"We don't need an influx of cash into our economy," she said gently.

He arched a disbelieving eyebrow. "Everyone can always use a boost in capital."

She shook her head. "No, the thing is, many of the people who retired here left high-paying corporate jobs. Hell, some of them were CEOs who sold their companies or left the management to their sons and daughters and came to Moon Island to escape their high-pressure jobs. They have more money than they'll ever spend."

"And the rest? The ones who've lived here all their lives?"

She shrugged. "They're happy. We have shrimpers who are third- and fourth-generation fishermen. We have local shop owners, restaurant workers, grocery store clerks. Basically everyone's job fulfills a need on the island. Selling souvenirs to tourists isn't a need. Neither is providing them entertainment. We have a comfortable living here. Some of us don't have much but we make it and we're happy."

"There is a certain weirdness to this whole place," Rafael said with an amused tone. "Like stepping into a time warp. I'm shocked that you have internet access, cable and cellular towers."

"We keep up," she said. "We just don't particularly care about getting ahead. There is a certain je ne sais quoi about our lifestyle, our people and our island. In a lot of ways it can't be described, only experienced. As you did for those weeks you were here."

"And yet you were going to walk away from your life here. For me."

She went still. "Yes, I've already said so. I mean I assumed I would have to make changes. You run a business. You have a home in New York. I could hardly expect you to give all that up and live here. I expected it to be an adjustment but I thought it—you—would be worth it."

"Given your passion for this island and the people here, I'm a little awed that you thought I was worth that kind of sacrifice."

"You sell yourself short, Rafael. Don't you think you're worth it? That someone could and should love you enough to give up important things to be with you?"

He averted his gaze, staring out over the water as if he had no answer. His body language had changed and he held himself stiffly. His jaw tightened and then he made an effort to relax.

"Maybe I've never met anyone who thought that much of me," he finally said.

"Again, you're associating with the wrong people. And you've definitely been dating the wrong women."

The mischievous tone in her voice wrung a smile out of him.

"Why do I get the feeling that I probably tried like hell to keep you at arm's length and you were having none of that?"

She frowned. "Not at all. You seemed…" Her expression grew more thoughtful. "You were definitely open to what happened between us. You certainly did your share of pursuing. Put it this way. I didn't have to try very hard to get past that stuffy exterior of yours."

He shook his head. "I'm beginning to think I have a double running around impersonating me. I know I keep saying this, but the man you describe is so far out of my realm of understanding that he seems a complete and utter stranger. If I didn't know better, I'd say I suffered the head injury before I arrived here. Not after."

"Does it appall you that much?"

He jerked his gaze to her. "No, that's not what I'm saying at all. It's not that I'm shamed or angry. It's hard to explain. I mean think for a moment of things you would never do. Think of something so not in line with your personality. Then imagine someone telling you that you did all those things but you can't remember them. You'd think they'd lost their mind, not that you'd lost yours."

"Okay, I can understand that. So it's not that you can't accept the person you were."

"I just don't understand him," Rafael mused. "Or why."

"Maybe you took one look at me and decided you had to have me or die," she said impishly.

He leaned sideways until their mouths were hovering just a breath apart. "Now that I can understand because I find I feel that way around you with increasing frequency."

She closed the remaining distance between them and found his lips in a gentle kiss. He kissed the bow of her mouth and then each corner in a playful, teasing manner, and every time she felt a thrill down to her toes.

"I have tea, but I can see you're not that interested," Mamaw said with a laugh.

Bryony pulled back and turned to see her grandmother standing outside the glass doors holding two tea glasses. "Of course I want your tea. It's the best in the south."

"Do I like it?" Rafael asked, a hint of a smile on his face.

Mamaw walked over and handed him a glass. "You sure do, young man. Said it was better than any of that fancy wine you drink in the city."

He gave her a smile that would have made most women melt on the spot. "Well, then if I said it I must have meant it." He took the glass and took a cautious sip.

Bryony took her own glass and sent Rafael an amused look. "It isn't spiked. I promise. You're looking at it like you expect it to be poisoned."

He took another sip. "It's good."

Mamaw beamed at him as if it were the first time she'd heard the compliment.

"Have a seat, Mamaw. We came to see you, not to be alone."

Her grandmother pulled up a chair and sat across from Bryony and Rafael. "Bryony tells me you were in a plane crash. That must have been traumatic for you."

Rafael nodded. "I don't remember much about the crash. I do have a few memories. Mostly of the aftermath and feeling relief that I was alive. But the rest is a blur. Including the weeks before the crash as I'm sure Bryony has told you."

Mamaw nodded. "It's a shame. Bryony was so upset. She was sure you'd pulled a fast one on her and left her alone and pregnant."

Heat crept up Bryony's neck. "Mamaw, don't."

"No, it's fine," Rafael said to Bryony. "I'm sure

she has anger toward me just like you did. There's no need for her to pretend differently."

Mamaw nodded. "I like a man who's honest and straightforward. Now that you're back and are trying to work things out with my grand-daughter, I think we'll get along just fine."

He smiled. "I hope so, Ms...." He stopped in midsentence and looked to Bryony for help. "What do I call her? I don't remember you telling me her name."

Bryony laughed. "That's because to everyone she's just Mamaw."

Mamaw reached forward and patted Rafael's leg. "There now, if that makes you uncomfort-able, you can call me Laura. Hardly anyone does. Just the mayor because he thinks it's unseemly for a man of his position to be so familiar with one of his constituents. His malarkey, not mine. He's a bit of an odd duck, but he's a decent enough mayor."

"Laura. It suits you. Pretty name for an equally pretty lady."

To Bryony's amusement, her grandmother's cheeks bloomed with color and for once she didn't have a ready comeback. She just beamed at Rafael like he'd hung the moon.

"Are things okay with you, Mamaw?" Bryony asked. "How have you been feeling and do you need us to get you anything while we're out?"

"Oh, no, child, I'm good. Silas came by while you were gone and took my grocery list to his nephew. He's got a job delivering groceries now. Just got his driver's license and he's excited to get to be driving everywhere. I keep expecting to hear of him getting into an accident with the way he zips around these roads but so far nothing's happened and not one of my eggs was broken, so I guess he's got it under control."

"You're taking your medicine every day like you're supposed to?"

Mamaw rolled her eyes and then looked toward Rafael. "One would think she was the grandmother and I was the ditzy young granddaughter. Mind you, it wasn't me who got herself pregnant. I know how to take *my* pills."

"Mamaw!"

She shrugged. "Well, it's true."

"Oh, God," Bryony groaned. "You're on fire today, aren't you. I should have just gone home."

Rafael chuckled and then broke into steady laughter. Bryony and her grandmother stared as he laughed so hard he was wiping at his eyes.

"You two are hilarious."

"Easy for you to say. She wasn't taking you to task for not using a condom," Bryony said sourly.

"It was next on my list," Mamaw said airily.

Rafael shook his head. "At least I can claim I have no memory of the event."

"It broke," Bryony said tightly.

"Now see, if you were taking your pills like you were supposed to, a broken condom wouldn't be an issue," Mamaw said.

Bryony stood and tugged at Rafael's arm. "Okay, I've had enough of let's embarrass the hell out of Bryony today. It's obvious Mamaw is feeling her usual sassy self, so let's go home. I'm starving."

Rafael laughed again and climbed out of his chair. He bent down to kiss Mamaw on the cheek. "It was a pleasure to reacquaint myself with you."

Fourteen

"Comfortable?" Rafael asked as he plumped a pillow behind Bryony's back.

Bryony reclined on the wicker patio lounger. She smiled up at Rafael and sighed. It was an absolutely beautiful day as only a fall day could be on the island. Still quite warm but without the oppressive heat and humidity of summer. The skies were brilliant blue, unmarred by a single cloud, and the salt-scented air danced on her nose as the soft music of the distant waves hummed in her ears.

"You're spoiling me," she said. "But by all means keep on. I'm not opposed in the least."

He sat at the opposite end of the lounger and

pulled her feet into his lap. He toyed with the ankle bracelet and then traced a finger over the arch of her foot.

"You have beautiful feet."

She shot him a skeptical look. "You think my feet are beautiful?"

"Well, yes, and you draw attention to them and your ankles with this piece of jewelry. I like it. You have great legs, too. A complete package."

"I don't think I've ever had my feet propped on a gorgeous guy's lap while he does an analysis of my legs and ankles before. It makes me feel all queenly."

He began to press his thumb into her arch with just enough force to make her moan.

"Isn't that how a man should make the mother of his child feel? Like a queen?"

"Oh, God, you're killing me. Sure, in theory, but how many guys really do? Of course, I've never been pregnant before so how would I know?"

He laughed. "I think you're supposed to pick up on the fact that I'm embracing this child as our child. Our creation. Together. I know it seems I've ignored his or her presence. We haven't discussed your pregnancy much, but I've thought of little else since I found out. It's kept me up at night. I lay there thinking how ill-prepared I am to be a father and yet I have this eager anticipation that eats at me. I start to wonder who the baby will look like. Whether it will be a son or a daughter."

Tears crowded her eyes and she felt like an idiot. But there was no doubt the longing in his voice hit her right in the heart and softened it into mush.

"Why do you think you're ill-prepared to be a father?" she asked softly.

He closed both hands around her foot and rubbed his thumbs up and down the bottom, pressing and massaging the sole, then moving up to her arch and on to the pads below her toes.

"I work to the exclusion of all else. I never go anywhere that I don't bring work with me. Most of my social events are work-related. There are times I sleep at my office. Just as many times I sleep on a plane en route to a meeting or to scope out a location for a new development. A child needs the attention of his parent. He needs their love and support. All I can really do is provide financially."

"I said this once already but you don't have

to stay the same person just because that's who you've always been. Parents make changes for their children all the time. I'm not any more prepared for parenthood than you are. I always imagined I'd wait until I was older."

He arched a brow. "Just how old are you? You make it sound like you're some teenager."

She laughed. "I'm twenty-five. Plenty old to have children but since until a few months ago I haven't had a serious relationship, and by serious I mean thinking of marriage and commitment, et cetera. I knew that having children was still some years away."

"It would seem we're both going to be handed parenthood before we thought we were ready."

"But would we really ever say we were ready? I mean who just announces one day, 'Okay, I'm ready for children'? I think even people who plan their pregnancies still have to be a little unprepared for the changes that occur with the arrival of a child."

"You're probably right. I think you'd make a great mother, though."

She cocked her head, flushed with pleasure at the compliment. "That means a lot that you'd say that, Rafael, but what makes you think so? I haven't exactly shown a lot of responsibility to this point."

"You are a loving and affectionate woman. Warm, spontaneous. Loyal and generous. And you're direct. You had no qualms about taking me on when you thought I'd wronged you. I can only imagine how fierce you would be in protection of our child."

"Do you know why I think you'd make a great father?"

His hands stilled on her foot and he glanced up at her.

"Because you admit your shortcomings," she said gently. "You know your faults. You acknowledge them. You're well aware of the areas where you'd need to change. Most people aren't that self-aware. I have no doubt that you'd be sensitive to your child's needs and make adjustments. There's nothing you can say to convince me that you wouldn't absolutely put your child first in your priorities."

He slid one hand up her leg to snag her fingers and then he squeezed. "Thank you for that."

"I still love you, Rafael."

The words slipped out. They were an ache in her heart that she had to let loose. Here in this moment, it was more than she could take, even though she'd sworn she wouldn't make herself vulnerable again until they had resolved his memory loss and their relationship. She simply had to tell him how she felt.

His eyes darkened. His hands were no longer gentle as he roughly pulled her up and toward him. She sprawled indelicately across his lap as he framed her face in his grasp. For a long moment, he stroked her cheek as he stared into her eyes.

Then he leaned his forehead against hers in a surprisingly tender gesture as he gathered her hand in his, trapped it between their chests.

"I had no idea how I'd feel when I asked you if you still love me yesterday. It was an idle curiosity. I had no idea the impact those words would make. I can't even explain it. How can I?"

"I had to tell you," she whispered. "I've been honest. I don't want to hold anything back. It's hard for me. I'm unused to being reserved. You deserve to know the truth. You're here. You're making the effort. The least I can do is meet you halfway. It was my pride that held me back before. I didn't want to humble myself or make myself vulnerable to you again, but holding back the words doesn't change anything."

He lowered his head and kissed her, forgoing his earlier gentle and playful smooches. His lips moved heatedly over hers, dragging breath from her then returning it, demanding it.

He tasted of the lemonade he'd served with the lunch he'd prepared. Tart and sweet and so hot. He licked over the seam of her mouth then plunged inward again as if determined to taste every part of her.

Always before, his lovemaking had seemed practiced and deliberate. Smooth and seductive. Now there was a desperation to his every caress and kiss, like he couldn't wait to touch her or to have her. Even as the differences plagued her, she gave herself over to this seemingly new man. It felt different. He was different.

"I want to make love to you, Bryony, but I want it to be for the right reasons. I want you to know I want you for the right reasons. Right now I couldn't care less about the past or what I do or don't remember. What I know is that right here, right now, I want to touch you and kiss you more than I want anything else."

As gracefully as she could manage when her

legs and hands were shaking, she got off his lap to stand before him. Then she reached down for his hand and slid her fingers through his.

"I want you, too," she said simply. "I've missed you so much, Rafe."

He rose unsteadily, his eyes dark and vibrant with desire. His usually calm composure seemed shaken and he raised a trembling hand to her cheek.

"Be sure of this, Bryony. Whatever happens today, whatever has happened in the past, what I remember or don't remember—it's not going to matter if you give yourself to me again. Now. If we do this now, we're starting over. New page. Fresh beginning."

She rubbed her cheek over his hand and closed her eyes. "I'd like that. No past. Just today. Here and now. You and me."

He wrapped an arm around her and urged her toward the door. They stumbled inside the cottage and she guided him toward her bedroom. Past the guest room where he'd slept the night before. Back to the place where they'd spent so many hours making love in the past.

He closed the door and she stood in front of him, suddenly shy and unsure. Though she'd made love with him countless times before, it seemed new. He seemed different. Maybe she herself was even different.

And then she laughed.

Her laughter startled him. He looked up and cocked his head to the side. "What's so funny?"

She closed her eyes and shook her head ruefully. "I was standing here thinking that this felt like the first time and I'm so terribly nervous but then I thought how ridiculous that was when I'm pregnant with your child, a testament to the fact that it's far from the first time for us."

His expression softened and he pulled her gently into his arms. "In a lot of ways this is our first time. I think we should treat it as such. I know I plan to reacquaint myself with your body. I want to touch and see every part of you. There'll be no rushing. I want to savor every moment and draw it out until we're both crazy."

She swayed toward him, feeling light-headed, as if she were a little drunk. He caught her to him and carefully walked her back until she met with the edge of the bed.

Silently he began to unbutton her shirt, taking his time as he worked down her body. When he was done, he carefully parted the lapels and pushed back and over her shoulders so that the material fell away and she stood in her jeans and bra.

"Pretty and delicate," he said as he fingered the lace that cupped the swell of her breast. "A lot like you. It suits you. I like you in pink."

"You don't fancy a siren in red or black?" she asked with a grin.

"No. Not at all. I like the softness of pink and how feminine it looks on you. Very girly."

He lowered his head to kiss the bare expanse of skin that peeked above the cup and then nuzzled lower, pushing down the lace ever so slightly until he was just a breath from her taut nipple.

Then he drew away. "I like girly."

"You are a tease," she said in a strained voice.

He reached down to unbutton her pants, loosening them and then pulling them down just enough to bare the swell of her belly.

To her utter shock, he went to his knees and molded her stomach with both hands. He gently caressed the bump and then pressed a kiss to her flesh.

It was an exquisitely tender moment and an image she'd never forget as long as she lived. This proud, arrogant man on his knees in front

of her, lavishing attention on their baby—
and her.

She gazed down, lovingly running her fingers
through his dark hair. He stared up at her and the
look in his eyes made her catch her breath.

Then he tugged at her jeans and slowly rolled
them over her hips and down her legs. When
they pooled at her feet, he lifted one leg, his
hands sliding up and down in a sensual caress.
He tugged the material free and then lifted her
other foot to completely remove the jeans.

"Matching lacy pink," he said just before pressing a kiss to the V of her underwear. "I like it. I
like it a lot."

Her legs trembled and butterflies fluttered
through her veins, around her chest and up into
her throat.

She wasn't self-conscious about her pregnant
body as many women were. In fact, she liked the
newfound lushness of her curves. In a lot of ways
she'd never looked better. Her skin glowed with a
healthy sheen. Her breasts had grown larger and
she was fascinated by the shape of her expanding
abdomen.

She hadn't really considered being worried over
Rafael's reaction to the changes in her body. If

she had, she would have worried in vain because he seemed entranced. Nothing in his actions told her he found her anything but desirable.

"You're beautiful," he said in a raw voice, almost as if he'd been privy to her thoughts.

Slowly he rose, sliding his hands up her body as he straightened to stand in front of her. Then he tangled his fingers in her hair and fit his mouth to hers.

She struggled for air but wouldn't retreat long enough to take a breath. She took every bit as much as he did, demanding more in return.

There was something markedly different between them. Their lovemaking had always been casual. Fun, a little flirty and laid-back. The Rafael who stood before her now was…different. It was in the way he looked at her, so dark and forbidding, as if he were set to devour her. As if he wanted her more than he'd ever wanted another woman.

Fanciful but there was definitely nothing casual about the way he touched and kissed her.

She liked the new Rafael. He was commanding and yet gentle and loving. Reverent.

He cupped one hand around her nape, his fingers pressing possessively on her neck as he pulled her into another bone-melting kiss. Then he nibbled a path down her jaw to her ear and sucked the lobe into his mouth. Each tug sent pulsating waves of desire low into her pelvis. Her muscles clenched and she tensed as a whispery sigh floated from her lips.

His mouth never leaving the sensitive column of her throat, he slipped his arms underneath hers and hoisted her upward so he could lift her onto the bed. He lowered her then hovered over her, his denim-clad knee sliding between her thighs.

He kissed her again, then reached up to brush the hair from her forehead, his touch so light and caressing that it sent a thrill coursing through her veins.

Once more he brushed his mouth across hers as if he hated to leave her even for the time it would take him to undress. But he stepped back and the fact that his hands shook as he pulled at his T-shirt endeared him to her all the more.

He stripped the shirt off, the muscles rippling across his chest and shoulders. He tossed it aside and then began undoing the fly of his jeans. She nearly moaned when he pulled both jeans and underwear down in one impatient shove.

The man was sexy. Cut like a flawless gem.

Toned. Fit. Lean but not too lean. He had enough bulk that told of his workout regimen.

Her gaze drifted downward to his groin and she sighed her appreciation as his erection jutted upward. Impatient for him to return to her, she shifted and leaned up on her elbows so she could better see him.

But then he was crawling back onto the bed, straddling her body. He put the flat of his palm on her chest and gently pushed her down onto the mattress. Then he carefully slipped the straps of her bra off her shoulders, nudging until the cups released her breasts.

He lifted her just enough that he could fit one hand underneath to unhook her bra and then he pulled it away and tossed it onto the floor.

For a long moment he stared down at her, his gaze drifting up and down her body then focusing on her, their eyes catching and holding.

"I'm burning the image of you into my memory," he said in a husky voice. "I don't want to ever forget again. I can't imagine how I ever did to begin with. What man when presented with such beauty could possibly let such a memory of it escape?"

Her heart went all fluttery again. It was hard

to breathe around him. When he wasn't sending shivers of delight over her flesh with his touch, he sent ripples of pleasure through her heart with his words.

"Kiss me," she begged softly.

"Just as soon as I've taken the last of your pink girly underwear off," he said with a smile.

His fingers danced down her sides and hooked into the lacy band of her panties and he tugged, moving backward as he pulled them down her legs.

This time he moved up the side of her and curled his arms around her, pulling her against him so her naked flesh met his. It was a shock. A delicious, decadent thrill. His hardness was cupped intimately in the V of her legs and her breasts pressed against the slightly hair-roughened surface of his chest.

As he kissed her, his hand roamed possessively down her back and over the swell of her buttocks and then around to cup her belly before drifting lower into the damp, sensitive flesh between her legs.

She moaned and arched forward as his fingers found her most sensitive points. His erection slid between her slightly parted legs, burning, rigid, branding her flesh.

She wanted him inside her, a part of her, after being so long without him. She stirred restlessly, clinging to him, spreading her legs wider to encourage him to take her.

He smiled against her mouth. "So impatient. I'm not nearly finished yet, little love. I want to make you crazy with pleasure before I make you mine again. So crazy that you'll scream my name when I slide into your warmth."

"I want you," she whispered. "So much, Rafe. I missed you. Missed holding you like this. Missed having you touch me."

He drew away and regarded her, his expression so serious that it touched something deep inside her. "I think somehow that I've missed you, too, Bryony. A part of me has. I don't think I could be so happy so quickly with you if we hadn't known each other before, if we hadn't been… close. Lovers. You feel so perfect next to me. I feel like I've opened the door into someone else's life because this feels nothing like mine and yet I want it so badly I can taste it. I can feel it."

She reached up and tugged him down into a

kiss, so moved by his words that her heart felt near to bursting.

"I don't want to wait. I need you now, Rafe. Please. Be inside me. Let me feel you."

He leaned over her body, pressing into her, his heat enveloping her. She savored the sensation of being mushed beneath him, of inhaling his scent so deeply that she could almost taste him.

"Are you sure you're ready, Bryony?"

Even as he spoke, he slid one finger inside her and rolled his thumb across her clitoris. She closed her eyes and gripped his arms until her fingers felt bloodless.

"Please," she whispered again.

He positioned himself and pushed the tiniest bit forward until he was barely inside.

"Open your eyes. Look at me, Bryony. Let me see you."

Her eyelids fluttered open and she met his gaze, so dark and sensual.

He slid forward again, just a bit, stroking her insides with fire. He seemed determined to draw out their reunion, to make it last.

She let her hands wander down his sides and she caressed up and down, encouraging him to complete the act.

He leaned down until their noses brushed and then he angled his mouth over hers just as he slid the rest of the way inside her welcoming body.

Tears burned her eyes. The knot in her throat was such that she couldn't speak. She didn't have words anyway to describe the sensation of being back with the man she loved after having thought she'd lost him.

He withdrew and thrust again, his mouth never leaving hers. He breathed her. She breathed him. Their tongues tangled, stroked and coaxed.

He let his body descend on her and planted his forearms into the mattress so that she wasn't completely bearing his weight as his hips rocked against hers.

It was much like the ocean waves, rolling forward then receding. Gentle and yet building in intensity. He was patient, much more patient than he'd ever been.

"Tell me if I hurt you," he said against her mouth. "Or if I'm too heavy for you."

In answer she wrapped both arms around him and hugged him tight. She slid one hand down to cup his firm buttocks as he undulated his hips against her.

"Tell me what you need," he whispered. "Tell me how to please you, Bryony."

Her hands ran up his back to his shoulders and then one slid to his nape, her fingers thrusting upward into his hair.

"You're doing just fine," she said dreamily. "I feel like I'm floating."

He dropped his head to suck lightly at her neck and then he nibbled to the curve of her shoulder and sucked again, harder this time until she was sure he'd leave a mark.

She hadn't had such a mark since she was a teenager, but strangely it thrilled her that she would have a reminder of his possession.

He groaned. "I'm sorry, Bryony. I can't— Damn it." He issued several more muffled curses that ended in a long moan as he increased his pace.

As soon as the intensity changed, the orgasm that had begun as a lazy, slow build escalated into a sharp coiling burn low in her abdomen. It rose and spread until she gasped at the tension.

She dug her fingers into his back, not knowing how else to handle the mounting pressure. She arched her buttocks off the bed, pushing him deeper inside her. He tensed and shuddered against her, reaching fulfillment while she was still reaching blindly for her own.

He pulled from her body, rolled to the side and slid his hand between her legs, caressing and stroking her taut flesh. He lowered his head to her breast and sucked her nipple into his mouth, laving it with his tongue as he pressed another finger inside.

His thumb rolled over her clitoris, his fingers worked deep and his mouth tugged relentlessly at her breast. Her surroundings blurred and the coiling tension suddenly snapped, unraveling at super speed.

"Rafael!"

Her back came off the mattress and her hand went to his hair, gripping, her fingers curling into his nape as she went rigid underneath him.

Her release was sharp. It was sweet. It was intense. It was one of the most shattering experiences of her life. She was left clinging to him, saying his name over and over incoherently as she came down.

He continued to stroke her, more gently than before, sweetly and comfortingly as she settled beneath him, her body quivering and shaking like she'd experienced a great shock.

Her mind couldn't quite put it all together yet. All she knew was that it had never been this way between them before. She was…shattered. There was no other way to put it. And completely and utterly vulnerable before him. Bare. Stripped.

He gathered her close, holding her tightly as they both fought for breath. His hands seemed to be everywhere. Caressing. Touching. Soothing. He kissed her hair, her temple, her cheek and even her eyelids.

The one thing that seemed to penetrate the haze that surrounded her was that however undone she was, he'd been equally affected.

She wrapped herself around him as tightly as he was wound around her, snuggled her face into the hollow of his neck and drifted into a fuzzy sleep, so sated that she couldn't have moved if she wanted to.

Fifteen

Bryony woke to warm kisses along her shoulder and hands possessively stroking her body.

"Mmm," she murmured as she lazily stretched.

"Oh, good, you're awake. I'd hate to think I was taking advantage of a sleeping woman."

She laughed. "Oh, I bet."

"I have a lot to make up for," he said.

He slid his mouth down the midline of her chest and then over the swell of one breast.

"You do?"

He traced the puckered crest of her nipple with his tongue and then sucked gently. He let go and looked up to meet her gaze. In the soft glow of her bedside lamp, she could see regret simmering in his eyes.

"Evidently I have no control when it comes to you. I wanted to make it good for you. I wanted it to last. I didn't take care of you very well. I guess it goes along with my selfish-bastard ways."

She rolled her eyes and lifted her palm to caress the side of his face. "If I had been any more satisfied I think I would have died. I like that I drove you a little wild."

He arched one eyebrow. "A little? I'm not sure that accurately describes the mind-numbing experience I had. I don't ever remember losing it like that with any other woman. Was it like that between us before?"

"No," she said softly. "Not like that."

"Better?"

"Definitely better."

"Ah, good then. I was starting to feel threatened by the self I couldn't remember."

She laughed and then so did he. It felt good for once to joke about an event that had altered the courses of both their lives.

"I'm hungry."

He lowered his mouth to her breast again. "So am I."

Laughing, she smacked his shoulder. "For food! It's been... What time is it anyway?"

He shrugged underneath her palm that had stilled on his shoulder. "Sometime in the wee hours of the morning. We slept a long time. You wore me out."

"Let's eat in bed and then…"

He arched an eyebrow as he stared lazily back up at her. "Then what?"

She smiled wickedly. "Then I'm going to have dessert."

"In that case—" he scrambled up, covers flying "—you stay here. I'll get us something to eat and be back in a minute."

She pulled the covers to her chin and snuggled into the pillows, smiling as he strode naked out of the bedroom. He didn't look at all abashed by his nudity. Confidence in a man was so sexy. She sighed and stretched, a dreamy smile spreading across her face.

Fifteen minutes later, Rafael returned with a tray holding two saucers. Piled on each was two grilled-cheese sandwiches. There were two glasses of leftover lemonade from lunch.

She sat up as he placed the tray over her lap and her mouth watered at the smell of the buttery grilled bread and melted cheese.

"Oh, this is perfect."

"Glad you approve. It was all I could think of that would be done this quickly," Rafael said as he climbed onto the bed. He sat cross-legged in front of her and reached for one of the sandwiches.

They ate, stealing glances, their gazes meeting and then ducking away. She was mesmerized by this unguarded side of Rafael. If possible she was more in love now—after only a few days—than she'd been before. It seemed like he was freer with her now.

She left half of one of the sandwiches and drank the lemonade down then waited patiently for him to finish his own food.

When he would have gotten up to remove the tray, she leaned forward and wrapped her hands around his wrists, holding him motionless. Then she shoved the tray off the bed. It landed with a clatter, the saucers and glasses rolling this way and that.

She kissed him. Not a sweet, nice-girl kiss. She gave him the naughty version that said *I'm about to have my wicked way with you.*

"Oh, hell," he groaned.

"Oh, yes," she purred just before she gave him a shove.

He fell back, sprawled on the bed, his eyes glowing with fierce excitement as she threw one leg over his knees and straddled him.

She reached down and wrapped her fingers around his straining erection and smiled. "I think it's time for dessert."

"Oh, damn…"

She lowered her mouth and ran her tongue around the tip of his penis. His breath hissed out, the sound explosive in the silence. His fingers tangled in her hair and he arched his hips.

"Bryony," he whispered.

She took him hard, loving and licking every inch of him. She wanted to give him as much pleasure as he'd given her. She wanted to show him her love—her heart.

She settled between his legs, her hair drifting down over his hips. His fingers gentled against her scalp and stroked lovingly as she continued making love to him.

He made low sounds of appreciation and of pleasure and he began thrusting upward, seeking more of her mouth. Finally it seemed to be too much for him to bear.

He grasped her shoulders and hauled her up his body until she straddled him.

She scooted up until his erection was against her belly and she carefully wrappped her fingers around his length. Instinctively she glanced back up, seeking direction. He held out his hands for her to grab and when she did, he pulled her toward him.

"Take me," he whispered. "I made you mine again. Now make me yours."

Oh, how seductive his husky words were. Prickles of anticipation licked over her skin like flames to dry wood. She rose up, using his hands to brace herself with. Their fingers slid together, twining, symbolic of their joining. She arched over him and he let one of her hands go long enough to position himself at her opening.

As soon as she began the delicious slide downward, he laced their fingers back again and she began the delicate mating dance of a woman reclaiming her man.

Before she'd never felt bold enough to take the initiative in their lovemaking. Rafael had always been the one to take control, had always seen to her pleasure before his own. And yet she preferred this man who wanted her so badly that he found his release before her, who was so lost in passion that he couldn't control his response. This man seemed more…real.

Now she delighted in teasing him, pleasuring him, taking control and driving him crazy with desire.

It was a heady, intoxicating feeling that only heightened as she watched him through half-lidded eyes.

He squeezed her hands and then took his away from hers. He caressed her hips then slid his palms up her sides to cup her breasts, toying and teasing her nipples as she undulated atop him.

His eyes glittering and his mouth tight, he lowered one hand, splayed it over her pelvis and dipped his thumb between their bodies to rub gently over her clitoris.

She flexed and spasmed around him and they both gasped. He stroked harder, finding a rhythm she responded to, and with his other hand, he caressed and plucked at her nipples, alternating until she was nearly mindless.

How quickly he'd turned the tables. Though she was on top, taking him in and out of her body at her leisure, his hands worked magic, finding all her sweet spots.

"Come for me, Bryony," he said. "I want to feel your heat around me as you come apart."

Her head fell back. Her entire body trembled. Her knees shook where they dug into the mattress. Beautiful, intense, vicious tension coiled low in her belly, spread to the spots he so expertly stroked and then it gathered and burst in all directions.

The force of her orgasm was staggering. She fell forward, but he was there to catch her. She braced her hands on his chest, not wanting to leave him, not wanting to stop until he found his own release, but she couldn't be still.

She writhed uncontrollably. All the while he held her and stroked his hands over her body as he whispered her name over and over in her ear.

She heard a sob, an exclamation of pleasure and knew it was herself, but it sounded so distant that it seemed impossible it could have come from her.

When her strength sagged from her, he simply held her hips and took over, thrusting upward into her still quivering body until he went tense underneath her.

Then he wrapped his arms around her, pulling her down until there was no space separating them. He thrust one last time and then they both went limp on the bed.

She was sprawled atop him. She probably resembled a dishrag, but she couldn't muster the energy to care.

He rubbed his hand up and down her back, down over her buttocks and then back up to tangle in her hair. He kissed her forehead and then ran his fingers through her hair again.

"That was incredible."

"Mmm-hmm," she agreed.

He stroked her arm in a lazy pattern. "What happened here, Bryony? It sure as hell wasn't just sex. I've had just sex before. This doesn't qualify."

"No," she said in a low voice. "It wasn't just sex."

"Then what was it?"

She raised her head and stared down into his eyes. "It was making love, Rafael. I love you. You loved me. I'd like to think that didn't just go away. Some things the heart knows even if the mind hasn't accepted it or has blocked it out."

"It scares the hell out of me that something this huge could be forgotten. I haven't loved anyone before."

"Never?"

He shook his head. "I'm sure I loved my parents in the beginning. I don't hate them now. I just don't think about them, the same way they don't think about me. I was an inconvenience. They were merely the people who gave me my DNA. It sounds cold, but it is what it is. I'm not saying that because I'm harboring some horrible psychological defect because my mommy doesn't love me. I'm merely saying that I've never deeply loved anyone and now that I supposedly have, I forgot it? It and nothing else?"

"Maybe finally falling in love was so traumatic for you that you blocked it out," she teased.

"I can't believe you can joke about this," he grumbled.

"Well, it's either laugh or cry and crying gives me a headache. Besides, you'll remember. I think you're already starting to. A lot of things are instinctive to you. You don't treat me like a stranger even though for all practical purposes I am. If you really thought I was unknown to you would you be in my bed sharing your deep, dark secrets?"

"Probably not," he admitted.

She leaned down to kiss him and then rested

her head on his shoulder again. "One day at a time, Rafe. It's all we can do and hope that each day brings us closer to the time you remember us."

He tightened his arm around her and kissed her forehead. "I'm not sure I deserve your sweetness or your patience, but I'm damn grateful for both."

Sixteen

When his BlackBerry rang first thing the next morning, Rafael knew by the ring tone who it was and he ignored it. Devon had called Cam in. Cam was calling to curse and yell at him that he was a moron who was thinking with his dick.

Cam was predictable if nothing else.

When his phone immediately began to ring again, Rafael cursed and leaned down as far as he could without loosening his hold on Bryony. He managed to drag his pants closer and fish the BlackBerry out. He hit the ignore button first and then hit the power button second.

His business could run without him for a couple of days. He paid many people very good money to think on their feet and be able to handle any situation that arose. It was time to give them the freedom to do what he'd hired them to do.

Oddly, in the past such an idea would make the control freak in him break out in hives. Now, he reasoned that he parted with good money so that he could occasionally enjoy a break.

Maybe Bryony was right. He didn't have to be the person he'd always been. Furthermore, she was right in that he would make sacrifices for his son or daughter.

He didn't want to be an absentee father. He didn't want to be like his own father, who thought being a provider was his only obligation to his family.

There was a hell of a lot more to parenthood than providing all the material necessities. Rafael wanted to be there for all the school plays, the soccer games. He wanted to be the one to put money under his kid's pillow when he lost a tooth and pretend that it was the tooth fairy.

He wanted to be a father. The best father he could be.

He gazed down at Bryony, whose head was pillowed on his shoulder. The morning sun shone on her skin, giving it a translucent, angelic glow.

She looked at peace. She looked content. She looked...loved.

Then his mind kicked in with a screaming *whoa*.

No way was he falling for this woman after only a few days.

But had it been just a few days? Or was he responding to the weeks they'd spent together before?

It could be she was right. On some level he remembered her, recognized her as the woman he'd chosen. But the woman he'd fallen in love with?

He'd always considered that love was like being struck by lightning. This odd sort of contentment didn't match with what he considered falling in love might feel like. He damn sure hadn't thought it could be so...easy.

Easy. Yeah. Love was complicated, wasn't it? No one managed to pull it off in a few days. It was the good sex talking.

But, no. Bryony had been right about one thing. It wasn't just sex. Calling it that cheapened it on some level. Reduced it to the level of flirtatious, sex-only relationships he'd had in the past. A quick romp in bed, send the woman on her way. Move on to the next.

Nothing about his past experiences came even close to the way he felt about Bryony or the way he felt about making love to her.

Last night had felt like something he'd been anticipating forever. A sense of homecoming that was so keen, it had nearly flattened him. He'd been ridiculously emotional, like he wanted to go around blurting out how he felt and crap. The mere idea should have humiliated the hell out of him, but it didn't.

Being forthright with Bryony just felt natural. She'd played it completely straight with him. He'd played it straight with her even when it had meant admitting or saying something that had hurt her.

It was weird being this honest and open with a woman—hell, with anyone. He trusted Ryan, Dev and Cam, but he never talked about intensely personal issues with them. Not that they wouldn't listen, but that wasn't the nature of their relationship.

His thoughts flickered back to the woman in his arms. Yeah, she did odd things to him. Made him want to do stuff, different stuff. Stuff that should have him running the other direction.

He sighed. This was a woman a man kept. Maybe he'd known that when he met her. Maybe it was true that a man just knew when he'd met the woman who would change everything for him.

Bryony was the marrying kind. Not the bed-'em-and-leave-'em-with-a-smile kind of woman. She had permanent written all over her sweet face.

She was…his. And hell if he was going to let her go. He didn't care if he ever remembered. He had enough pieces of the puzzle to know that she belonged with him. They had a lot to work out—what new couple didn't? They'd jumped ahead a few steps in the relationship with her being pregnant, but it wasn't anything they couldn't work out.

The more he settled the matter in his mind, the more convinced he became that this was right. She was right. Bryony. Their baby. Him. A family. He could have it all.

The resort.

He grimaced. It hung over him like a dark cloud. It was the one thing standing between him and Bryony. She swore he had promised her he wouldn't develop the land, which made absolutely no sense. Why buy it at all? He certainly didn't have need of a private expanse of beach for personal use.

A hell of a lot rode on this deal.

There had to be some way to convince her and the rest of the people on the island that one resort wouldn't change their way of life.

It was either that or he had to go back to his partners—and friends—and investors and pull the plug on the entire thing. He would lose a hell of a lot of money, but worse than that, he'd lose credibility, future backing and his standing in the business community.

All because of a promise he couldn't remember making.

Bryony stirred in his arms and his grip tightened possessively around her. Before she could open her eyes, he pulled her close and kissed her lingeringly.

She sighed as her eyelashes fluttered, then her warm brown eyes found his and she smiled. "That's a nice way to wake up."

"I was thinking the same thing," he murmured.

"What time is it?"

"Seven."

She yawned and snuggled closer to him. "Plenty of time."

"Plenty of time for what?"

"To do whatever we want or nothing at all."

He chuckled. "I like your attitude."

"Any idea what you'd like to do today?"

"Yeah, actually. I thought you could take me around the island. Private tour. Show me what makes it so special to everyone who lives here. I can't remember the last time I went to a beach just to see and enjoy the sights and sounds."

She leaned her head back and frowned. "You work entirely too hard. Maybe your accident was a blessing in disguise. If it causes you to slow down and reevaluate then it's a good thing."

"I wouldn't have put it that way exactly. I'm not sure nearly dying is the kind of wake-up call anyone wants," he said dryly.

She touched his cheek. "But would you be thinking the way you're thinking now if it hadn't happened?"

He sighed. "Maybe not. Maybe you're the reason for my reevaluation. Ever think of that?"

She smiled and leaned up to kiss him. "I'll take that explanation. I prefer it over thinking about you dying anyway."

"You and me both," he muttered.

"Tell you what. You hit the shower. I'll cook breakfast. Then I'll take my bath and we'll head out. The weather is supposed to be gorgeous all week. We can pack a picnic and eat out on the beach."

"I've got a better idea. How about we shower together then I'll help you cook breakfast. I cook a mean piece of bacon."

She laughed and he sucked in his breath at the love shining in her eyes as she stared up at him. No one had ever looked at him like that.

Then her expression grew serious as she stroked her palm over his unshaven jaw. "I love you, Rafe. I don't want to make you uncomfortable. I don't expect anything in return. But now that I've told you I can't not keep saying it. I look at you and it just bursts out."

He captured her hand and pulled it to his mouth, his heart thudding against the wall of his chest. "I like you saying it," he said hoarsely. "It means… It means everything to me right now."

She pulled away, joy lighting her eyes. Eyes he could drown in. Her eyes were so expressive. They reflected her mood so perfectly. Sad, angry, happy. You only had to look into her eyes to know exactly what she was thinking.

She crawled over him, giving him a good view and feel of her soft curves. It was all he could do not to haul her back and make love to her all over again.

When her feet hit the floor, she turned back and held out her hand. "How about that shower?"

.He stared at her profile for a long moment, committing to memory just how she looked bathed in morning sunlight, her gently rounded abdomen, the swell of her breasts and the wild curls that spilled down her back.

This was his. His woman. His child.

"Do you have any idea how beautiful you are?"

She flushed, her face grew pink, but her eyes lit up until they were as bright as the sunlight pouring into her room.

"I do now."

He grinned at her cheeky response. "Let's go hit the shower."

Seventeen

"You've done a good thing, Mr. de Luca," Silas Taylor said as they stood on the patio of Laura's house.

Bryony's grandmother had invited everyone over for tea and lemonade and for some of her famous peanut butter cookies. And by everyone, she meant whomever happened to wander by.

Such a thing baffled Rafael, who was used to strict guest lists and checking invitations at the door. Laura didn't seem to mind. In fact, the more guests that meandered through, the more delighted she seemed to be.

There was no entertainment. Conversation drifted from one mundane topic to the next or people just stood around, enjoying the day and inquiring as to the health of yet another islander who was either family, friend or both.

"My investors probably wouldn't agree," Rafael said dryly as he turned his attention back to the sheriff.

Silas shrugged. "They'll find something else to invest in. Those kind always do. People are always looking for places to put their money and there are always people willing to take it. Seems to me it wouldn't be that hard to figure it out."

Rafael wanted to laugh. Or shake his head. Months of financial analysis, blueprints being drawn up, investors courted, endless planning on his and Ryan, Devon and Cam's parts all reduced to a few words so casually tossed out.

"That may be so, but I lose credibility and re-spect in the process," Rafael said evenly. "Next time I want their backing, they won't be so will-ing to give it."

"And what will you gain?" Silas asked as he looked in Bryony's direction. Bryony, who stood in a small group of people looking so damn beau-tiful that it made Rafael's teeth ache. "Seems to me you gain far more than you lose." With that, Silas slapped him on the shoulder.

"Something to think about, my boy."

Then he walked away, leaving Rafael to shake his head again. Boy. He wanted to laugh. Granted the sheriff was at least thirty years older than Rafael, but no one had called him a boy since he'd been a boy.

Time was running out. His BlackBerry was full of voice-mail notifications and missed calls, and his inbox was bursting. His week would soon be up, and Dev would come down with Ryan and Cam to kick Rafael's ass.

For the past several days, Rafael had willfully ignored everything but Bryony and their time together. They'd spent every waking moment walking the beach, cooking together, laughing together, talking of nothing and everything.

They made love, they ate, they made love some more. There was an urgency he couldn't explain, almost as if he wanted to cram a lifetime into as few days as possible because he feared it would all slip away from him.

Tomorrow decisions had to be made. He couldn't hold them off any longer. He still had no idea what he would do, but he couldn't—wouldn't—lose Bryony over a resort. Over money.

"Can I get you something, Rafael?"

Rafael turned to see Bryony's grandmother smiling at him. He smiled back and shook his head. "No, I'm okay. Don't let me keep you from your guests."

"Oh, they're fine. Besides, you're a guest, too. How are you liking your stay so far?"

Again Rafael's gaze found Bryony. This time she lifted her head as if sensing that he watched her and her face lit up with a gorgeous smile.

"I'm enjoying it very much. I'm only sorry I can't remember when I was here before."

Laura stared thoughtfully at him for a long moment and then put her hand on his shoulder. "Maybe it's better that you don't."

She patted him and after offering those cryptic words, she turned to talk to another group of people.

Rafael shoved his hands in his pockets and turned to stare out over the water. He hadn't ever been someone who practiced avoidance, but he knew that was precisely what he was doing. Here, it was as if he existed in a bubble. Nothing could intrude or interfere, but the outside world was still there, just waiting. The longer he put off the inevitable, the more he dreaded it.

"Rafael, is something wrong?"

Bryony's soft voice slid over him at the same time her hand slipped through his arm and she hugged herself up to his side.

He disentangled his arm from her grasp just long enough to wrap it around her waist and then pulled her in close again.

"No, just thinking."

"About?"

"What has to be done."

Instead of pressing him for answers as he thought she might, she said, "Why don't we take off, go for a long walk? Mamaw won't mind. She's having fun being the center of attention. She won't even notice we've gone."

Unable to resist, he leaned down to kiss her brow. She was so in tune with his moods. It shouldn't have surprised him that she could read him so easily. He'd found that he could pick up on the nuances of her moods just as quickly. He anticipated her reactions much like she did his own.

It was something he imagined a couple doing after years of marriage.

When he drew away, she took his hand and

tugged him toward the stone path leading through the garden and down the dune onto the sand.

Sand slid over his toes but he found he didn't mind as much as he had when he first started wearing these ridiculous flip-flops.

They ventured closer to the water that foamed over the sand. Soon the cool waves washed over their feet, and Bryony smiled her delight as they danced back to avoid a larger one from getting them too wet.

Soon Laura's and Bryony's cottages were distant points behind them as they approached the land that he'd purchased from her.

"My father used to bring me here," she said. "He used to tell me that there was nothing greater than owning a piece of heaven. I feel like I've let him down by selling it."

Rafael grimaced feeling even guiltier over his part in the whole thing. It didn't matter that if it hadn't been him it would have been someone else. She could no longer afford the taxes and if someone hadn't bought it, eventually the land would have been seized for taxes owed. Either way it would no longer belong to her.

But you have the power to give it back to her. The thought crept through his mind, whispering to him. It was true. He owned the land. Not his company. Not his partners. He'd purchased the land outright. The building of the resort and development of the land was what he'd brought investors in for.

"I love you," she said as she squeezed his hand.

He looked curiously at her, startled by her sudden affection.

She smiled. "You just looked like you needed that today."

He stopped and pulled her into his arms, brushing a thick strand of her hair from her eyes as the wind blew off the water. "I did need that. I shouldn't be surprised that you always know just what to say." He took in a deep breath. "I love you, too, Bryony."

Her eyes went wide with shock and then filled with tears. Her body trembled against him. "You remember?" she whispered.

He shook his head. "No, but it doesn't matter. You said I loved you then. I know I love you now. Isn't now all that matters?"

Wordlessly she nodded.

"The whole story doesn't seem so crazy anymore," he admitted. "I couldn't accept that I fell in love with you in a matter of weeks and yet here I am in love with you after only a few days."

"Are you sure?"

He smiled but his heart clenched at the hope and fear in her eyes. She seemed so worried that he'd change his mind or that he wasn't really sure of himself or his feelings.

He tipped her chin up and leaned down to brush a kiss across her lips. "I've handled this whole thing so clumsily. I don't have any experience with telling a woman I love her. I imagine there were more romantic ways of doing it but I simply couldn't *not* say it any longer."

"Oh, Rafe," she said, her eyes bright with love and joy. "You've made me so happy today. I've been so afraid and unsure. I hate being uncertain more than anything else. The not knowing just eats at you until you're a nervous wreck."

"I'm sorry. I don't want you to worry. I love you."

She wrapped her arms around his neck and hugged him to her. "I love you, too."

He slowly pulled her arms away until he held her in front of him. She looked a little worried at the sudden seriousness of his expression and he tried to soften his features to reassure her.

But he couldn't really offer her any reassurance. Not yet.

"I need to leave tomorrow," he said grimly.

Her expression went blank and her mouth opened but nothing came out. "Wh-why?" she finally stammered out.

"I need to go back and work things out with my partners and our investors. I've avoided it for as long as I can. I can't do so any longer. I wanted you to know how I felt before I leave. I don't want you to have any doubts that I'll come back this time."

Uncertainty flickered across her face and her eyes went dim. He could tell she didn't entirely trust him and he couldn't blame her. Not after what had happened last time.

"You could come with me," he said. He was grasping at straws, anything to allay her fears. "We wouldn't have to be gone long. A few days at most. I know you don't like to be away from... here."

She reached for him, her hands clutching at his arms as she looked up at him, her eyes so earnest. "I don't like to be away from *you,* Rafe. You. Not here. Or there. Or anywhere."

"Then come with me. I won't lie to you, Bryony.

I don't know if I can fix this. All I can do is promise to try."

She let her hands slide down to grip his, so tight that her knuckles went white. "I believe in you."

He crushed her to him and buried his face in her hair. She made him want to be the man she was so convinced he already was.

"You'll come with me?"

"Yes, Rafe. I'll come with you."

She pulled away and he laced their fingers together, holding their hands between them.

"No matter what happens, Bryony, I love you and I want this to work out between us. I need for you to trust in that."

"I do trust you. You'll fix this, Rafe. I know you will."

He smiled then, feeling some of the anxiety lift away. He could breathe easier. The idea of expressing his feelings had given him a sense of uneasiness, but now that he'd done it, he realized it had been harder not to tell her what was in his heart even if his head still screamed that this was all wrong.

He'd spent a lifetime of listening to his head

and being ultra-practical. Maybe it was time he threw a little caution to the wind and let his heart lead for once.

Eighteen

Bryony's phone rang in the middle of the night. She pried herself from Rafael's arms and reached blindly for the phone on her bedside table.

"Hello?"

"Bry, it's Silas. You need to come to the hospital. It's your grandmother."

Bryony scrambled up, shaking the fuzz of sleep from her eyes. "Mamaw? What happened?"

"She had one of her spells. Blood sugar dropped. She called me and I couldn't understand a word she was saying so I rushed over and took her to the hospital."

Dear Lord, and she and Rafael had slept through it all.

"Why didn't someone come over and tell me?" she demanded.

"There wasn't a need to alarm you if it turned out to be nothing. I still think it's nothing but the nurse insisted I contact you so you could come down and sign some paperwork. They just want the insurance stuff squared away. You know these damn hospitals. Always wanting their money," Silas grumbled.

"Of course, I'll be right there."

Bryony hung up to see Rafael sitting up in bed, a look of concern on his face.

"Is Laura all right?"

Bryony grimaced. "I don't know. She's a diabetic and she doesn't always take care of herself. Sometimes she doesn't always take her insulin and at other times she doesn't eat when she should. I never know if she's in insulin shock or on the verge of diabetic coma."

"I'll go with you," he said as he hurried from the bed.

Twenty minutes later, they strode into the small community hospital. Silas met them in the main hallway.

"How is she?" Bryony asked anxiously.

"Oh, you know your grandmother. She's as mad

as a wet hen at having to stay overnight. She didn't even want to go to the hospital. I made her drink some orange juice at the house and she came right around but I thought she ought to be checked out anyway. She's not speaking to me as a result."

Bryony sighed. "Where is she now?"

"They moved her out of the emergency room to observation. They won't release her until they know for sure they have someone to watch over her for the next twenty-four hours."

"Take us to her," Bryony said.

As Silas predicted, Mamaw was in a fit of temper and ready to go home. The doctor was attempting to lecture her on the importance of not missing a meal and Mamaw's lips were stretched tight in irritation.

She brightened considerably when Bryony and Rafael walked through the door but glowered in Silas's direction.

Bryony went to the bed and kissed her grandmother's cheek. "Mamaw, you scared me."

Mamaw rolled her eyes. "I'm fine. Any fool can see that. I'm ready to go home. Now that you're here, they should let me go. They seem to think I need a babysitter for the next little while."

"Glad to see you're all right, Laura," Rafael said as he bent to kiss her cheek.

Mamaw smiled and patted Rafael's cheek. "Thank you, young man. Sorry to drag you and my granddaughter out of bed at this hour. Pregnant women need their rest, but no one but me seems to be concerned with that little tidbit."

"Is she okay to go home, Doctor?" Bryony asked, directing her attention to the physician standing to the side.

The doctor nodded. "She knows what she did wrong. I doubt it'll do any good to tell her not to do it again, but she's fine otherwise. You'll need to keep an eye on her for the next twenty-four hours and check her blood sugar every hour. Make sure she eats properly and takes her insulin as directed."

"Don't worry. I will," Bryony said firmly. "Can we take her home now or does she need to stay?"

"No, as long as she goes home with someone, she's free to leave as soon as we get her discharged. That'll take a few minutes so make yourself comfortable."

Mamaw shooed the doctor away with a scowl and then stared pointedly at Silas, who still stood by the door. With a sigh, Silas nodded in Bryony's direction and walked out.

Bryony shook her head in exasperation. "When are you going to stop being such a twit to him, Mamaw? He's crazy about you and you know darn well you're just as crazy about him."

"Maybe when he stops treating me like I'm incapable of taking care of myself," she grumbled.

Bryony threw up her hands. "Maybe he'll stop when you prove that you can. You know better than to skip meals, especially after taking your insulin."

Rafael picked up Mamaw's hand and gave her a smooth smile. "You cannot fault a man for wanting to ensure the safety of the woman he loves. It's a worry we never get over. We always want to protect her and see to her well-being."

Mamaw looked a little gob-smacked. "Yes, well, I suppose…" She cleared her throat and glanced at Bryony again. "I thought you two were leaving in the morning."

"Rafael will have to go without me," Bryony said brightly. "You come first, Mamaw. I'm not leaving you alone after promising the doctor I'd look after you."

Rafael slid his hand over Bryony's shoulder.

"Of course, you should stay. Hopefully my business in the city won't take long and I'll be back to see my two favorite women again."

"You have a smooth tongue, young man," Mamaw said sharply. Then she smiled. "I like it. I like it a damn lot. If Silas were that smooth, I'd probably have already said yes to his marriage proposal."

Bryony's mouth popped open. "Mamaw! You never told me Silas has asked you to marry him. Why haven't you said yes?"

Mamaw smiled. "Because, child, at my age I'm entitled to a few privileges. Making my man stew a little is one of them. If I said yes too quickly he'd take for granted my affection for him. A man should never take his woman for granted. I aim to make sure he always knows how lucky he is to have me."

Rafael broke into laughter. "You are a very wise woman, Laura. But do me a favor. Let Silas off the hook soon. The poor guy is probably miserable."

"Oh, I will," Mamaw said airily. "At my age I can't afford to wait too long."

Bryony squeezed her grandmother's hand. "I'll stay over with you at your house. I know you don't like to be away from your home for very long."

Mamaw's expression became troubled. "I don't want to interfere in your plans. You two have had enough problems without me adding to them."

Rafael put a finger to his lips to shush her. "You're no burden, Laura. I'll be back before either of you know it and then Bryony and I can plan our future together."

Bryony's heart pounded a little harder. It was the first time he'd spoken of their future—as in a life—together. He'd told her he loved her. She believed him. But she'd been greatly unsure of where that put them. There were still a lot of obstacles to overcome.

The fact that he seemed committed to them being together long-term sent relief through her veins.

Just then a nurse walked in with discharge papers and began the task of taking Mamaw's IV out and discussing the doctor's orders with her.

A half an hour later, they had Mamaw bundled into the car and were on their way back to her cottage.

Once Bryony got her grandmother into bed, she

walked back into the living room where Rafael waited. She went into his arms and savored the hug he gave her.

"Crazy night, huh?" he said.

She drew away. "Yeah. Sorry I won't be able to go with you. I don't think I should leave Mamaw even if she says she's fine."

"No, of course you shouldn't," he agreed. "I'll call you from New York and let you know how things are going. Hopefully I can be back in a few days. I have motivation to get this done."

She arched a brow. "Oh?"

He smiled. "Yeah, a certain pregnant lady will be waiting for me to return. I'd say that's pretty powerful incentive to get everything wrapped up so I can get my butt back on a plane."

"Yeah, well, Rafael? This time don't get into an accident. I'd really like not to have to wait months to see you again."

He tweaked her nose. "Smart-ass. If it's all the same, I have no desire to ever crash again. Once was enough. I know how lucky I am to be alive. I plan to stay that way for a long time to come."

She leaned into him and wrapped her arms around him. "Good. Because I have plans for you that are going to take a very, very long time to fulfill."

He gave her a questioning look. "Just how long are we talking about?"

"As long as you can keep up with me," she murmured.

"In that case, it's going to be a very long time indeed."

She kissed him and then reluctantly pulled away. "You should probably go back home so you can shower and get packed. It'll be light soon and you'll need to be down to catch the ferry. Rush-hour traffic going into Houston is a bitch and you're going to be hitting it at a bad time."

"You sure you're okay with me driving your car?"

She laughed. "The question should be whether it's going to hurt your pride to drive my MINI. I could always have Silas drive you to Galveston and you could get a car service to the airport."

He shook his head. "Your car is fine. Right now my only concern is that it gets me there so I can hurry up and return to you."

She rested her forehead on his chest. "I'll miss you, Rafe. I won't lie, the idea of you leaving panics me because I keep thinking of the last time I said goodbye to you thinking I'd see you again in a few days."

He cupped her face and tilted her head back so she looked up at him. "I'm coming back, Bryony. A plane crash and the loss of my memory didn't keep us apart last time."

"I love you."

He kissed her. "I love you, too. Now go get some rest. I'll call you when I land in New York."

Nineteen

"It's about damn time you got your ass up here," Cam said grimly as he got out of his car in passenger pickup at LaGuardia and strode around to help Rafael with his bags. "Devon's been in a snit ever since you left. Your delaying the groundbreaking just pissed him off even more. Copeland has got him over a barrel with this whole marrying-his-daughter thing. Ryan has been stewing over private investigator reports. I swear no one's head is where it should be right now. Except mine. It's obvious that any time a woman's involved disaster follows," he said sourly.

"Cam?" Rafe said mildly as he opened the door to the passenger side.

Cam yanked his gaze up and stopped before climbing into the driver's seat. "What?"

"Shut the hell up."

Cam got into the car grumbling about flaky friends and vowing all the while never to mix business and friendship again. Rafael rolled his eyes at his friend's consternation, considering that the four had always done business together.

"So what the hell is going on, Rafael? Dev says you've gotten cold feet."

"I don't have cold feet," Rafael growled. "I just think there has to be another way of making this deal go through that doesn't involve using the property on Moon Island."

Cam swore again. He went silent as traffic got snarled and he expertly weaved in and out, making Rafael white-knuckle his grip on the door handle.

Anyone riding with Cam deserved hazard pay. Not that he drove often. Cam almost always had a driver and it wasn't because he was too good to drive himself. Quite simply he was so busy that he utilized every moment of his time to conduct his business affairs and if he had a driver, he had that much more time to work.

Rafael figured Dev must have leaned on him

pretty hard to get him to drive himself to the airport to pick up Rafael.

"So you still don't remember anything?" Cam asked when they'd cleared one particularly nasty snarl.

"No. Nothing."

"And yet you believe her? Have you even started the process for paternity testing yet?"

"It doesn't matter what happened before. I love her now," Rafael said quietly.

There was dead silence in the car. Only the sounds of traffic and car horns penetrated the thick silence inside the car.

"And the resort deal?" Cam finally asked.

"There has to be something we can work out. It's why I'm here. We have to fix this, Cam. My future depends on it."

"How nice of you to be so concerned about your future," Cam muttered. "Nothing about the rest of ours, though."

"Low blow, man," Rafael bit out. "If I didn't give a damn about you and Ryan and Dev, I wouldn't be here. I would have just called off the whole damn thing and told all the investors to go to hell."

Cam shook his head. "And you wonder why I've sworn off women."

"Planning to play for the other team?" Rafael asked for a grin.

Cam shot him the bird and glowered. "You know damn well what I mean. Women are good for sex. Anything more and a man might as well neuter himself and be done with it."

Rafael chuckled. "You know I look forward to the day that I get to shove those words down your throat. Even better, I can't wait to meet the woman who does it for you."

"Look, I just don't understand what's changed. Four months ago you were on top of the world. You got what you wanted. And now suddenly it's not what you want."

They pulled to a stop in front of Rafael's apartment building. Rafael turned to Cam. "Maybe what I want has changed. And how the hell would you know that I got what I wanted four months ago? I didn't see you until I woke up in a hospital bed after the plane crash."

Cam shook his head. "You called me the day before you left. You were all but crowing. Said you'd closed the land deal that day and that next you were going to be on a plane back to New

York. I asked if you'd had a good vacation since you'd been gone for four damn weeks. You told me that some things were worth the sacrifice."

Rafe went still. Suddenly it was hard to get air into his lungs. His chest squeezed painfully as pain thudded relentlessly in his head.

"Rafael? You okay, man?"

Still images flashed through his head like photos. The pieces of his lost memory shot out of a cannon. Random. Out of order. It all hurled at him at supersonic speed until he was dizzy and disoriented.

"Rafe, talk to me," Cam insisted.

Rafael managed to open the car door and stumble out onto the curb. He put a hand back toward Cam when his friend would have gotten out, too.

"I'm fine. Leave me. I'll call you later."

He hauled his luggage out of the trunk and then walked mechanically toward the entrance. His doorman swung open the glass doors and offered a cheerful greeting.

Like a zombie, Rafael got into the elevator, clumsily inserted his card and nearly fell when the elevator began its ascent.

Memories of the first time he saw Bryony. Making love—no, having sex with her. The day at the closing agent's office when Bryony had signed over her land and he'd given her the check. Of the day he'd told her goodbye.

It all came back so fast his head spun trying to catch up.

He was going to be sick.

The elevator doors opened and it took him a full minute to force himself inside his apartment. Leaving his luggage inside the doorway, he staggered toward one of the couches in the living room, so sick, so devastated that he wanted to die.

He slumped onto the sofa and lowered his head to his hands.

Oh, God, Bryony would never forgive him for this.

He couldn't forgive himself.

"Mamaw, would it really be so terrible if they built a resort here?" Bryony asked quietly as the two women sat on Mamaw's deck.

Mamaw glanced over at Bryony, her eyes soft with love. "You're taking on too much, Bryony. You have to decide what's best for you. It's not your responsibility to make the entire island happy. If this resort is coming between you and Rafael, you have to decide what is the most important to you. Is it making everyone here happy? Or is it being happy yourself?"

Bryony frowned. "Am I being unreasonable to hold him to a promise he made? It seemed so simple then, but apparently he has business partners—close friends of his—and investors counting on him. This is how he makes his living. And I'm asking him to give all that up because we're all afraid that our lives will change."

Mamaw nodded. "Well, that's something only you can answer. We've been lucky for a lot of years. We've been overlooked. Galveston gets all the tourists. We stay over here and no one ever comes calling. But we can't expect that to last forever. If Rafael doesn't build his resort, someone else will eventually. We'd probably be better off if Rafael builds it because he at least has met the people here and he knows where they're coming from. If some outsider comes in, he won't give a damn about you or me or anyone else here."

"I don't want everyone to hate me," Bryony said miserably.

"Everyone won't hate you," Mamaw said gently. "Rafael loves you. I love you. Who else do you want to love you?"

Suddenly she felt incredibly foolish. She closed her eyes and slapped her head to her forehead. "You know what? You're right, Mamaw. It's my land. Or it was. Only I should have the right to decide who I sell it to and what they do with it. If the other people here wanted things to remain the way it was so badly then they could have banded together to buy the land. It was okay when they didn't have to foot the tax bill. They were more than happy to tell me what I could or couldn't do with my own land."

Mamaw chuckled. "That's the spirit. Get angry. Tell them to piss off."

"Mamaw!"

Her grandmother laughed again at Bryony's horrified expression.

"You've tied yourself in knots for too long, honey. First you were upset that he left. Then you were convinced he left you for good. Then you found out you were pregnant and you grieved for him all over again. Then he came back and you were happy. Don't give it up this time. This time you can do something about it."

Bryony leaned forward and hugged her grandmother. "I love you so much."

"I love you, too, my baby."

"Don't think I'm not going to turn these words back on you about Silas."

Her grandmother laughed and pulled away. "You leave Silas to me. He knows I'll come around sooner or later and he seems content to wait until I decide to quit making him miserable. I'm old. Don't begrudge me my fun."

"I don't want to be away from you. I want you to see your great-grandchild when he's born."

Mamaw sighed in exasperation. "You act like we'd never see each other anymore. Your Rafael is as rich as a man can get. If he can't afford to fly you to see me, then what good is he? You should ask for a jet as a wedding present. Then you can go where you want and when you want."

Bryony shook her head. "You're such a mess. But you're right. I'm just being difficult because I hate change."

Mamaw squeezed her hand. "Change is good for all of us. Never think it isn't. It's what keeps us young and vibrant. Change is exciting. It keeps life from getting stale and predictable."

"I suppose I should call Rafael and tell him to go ahead with the resort. It'll be such a load off him I'm sure."

"Better yet, why don't you get on a plane and

go see him," Mamaw said gently. "Some things are better said in person."

"I can't leave you. I promised the doctor—"

"Oh, for heaven's sake. I'll be fine. I'll call Silas over to drive you to the airport. If it makes you feel any better, I'll have Gladys come over and stay with me until Silas comes back."

"Promise?"

"I promise," Mamaw said in exasperation. "Now get on the internet and figure out when the first available flight is to New York."

Twenty

Bryony got into the cab and read off the address to the driver. She was nervous. More nervous than she'd ever been in her life. How ridiculous was it that she had to get Rafael's address from the papers from the sale of the land. She hadn't known. It hadn't been covered in ordinary conversation.

She was truly flying solo because Rafael hadn't answered his cell phone or his apartment phone. A dreaded sense of déjà vu had taken hold but she forced herself not to descend into paranoia. He had every reason the first time not to answer her calls given that he was in the hospital recovering from serious injuries.

Still, old feelings of helplessness and abandonment were hard to get rid of and the more times she tried to call with no response, the more anxious she became.

The ride was long and streetlights blinked on in the deepening of dusk. The city took on a whole different look at night. It seemed so ordinary and horribly busy during the day. People everywhere. Cars everywhere. Not that there wasn't an abundance of both at night, but the twinkling lights on every building lit up the sky and gave the skyline a beautiful look.

When the cab pulled up in front of Rafael's building she got out, paid the fare and then stood staring at the entrance. She shivered. Of course she'd forgotten a coat. It still hadn't been ingrained in her that while it was warm where she lived, it was cold in other places. And she'd been in such a hurry to get to Rafael, she hadn't bothered with more than an overnight bag and a few necessities.

She started toward the door when a man brushed by her. She frowned. He looked familiar. Ryan? One of Rafael's friends. Ryan Beardsley. Maybe he could at least get her inside since Rafe wasn't answering his phone.

"Mr. Beardsley," she called as she hurried to catch him before he disappeared inside.

Ryan stopped and turned, a frown on his face. When he saw her, the frown disappeared but neither did he smile.

"I don't know if you remember me," she began.

"Of course I remember you," he said shortly. "What are you doing here? And for God's sake, why aren't you wearing a coat?"

"It was warm when I left Texas," she said ruefully. "I came to see Rafael. It's important. He hasn't been answering his phone. I need to see him. It's about the resort. I wanted to tell him it was okay. I don't care anymore. Maybe I never should have. But I don't want him to mess things up for you or his investors or his other friends."

Ryan looked at her like she was nuts. "You came here to tell him all that?"

She nodded. "Do you know if he's home? Have you heard from him? I know he's busy. Probably more so now than ever, but if I could just see him for a minute."

"I'll do you one better," Ryan muttered. "Come on. I'll take you up to his apartment. Devon should already be here. We haven't heard from him since he arrived."

Bryony's eyes widened in alarm.

"Now don't go looking like that," Ryan soothed. "Cam dropped him off and he was fine. He's probably just busy trying to dig himself out of this mess he's gotten himself into."

He took Bryony's arm and tugged her toward the door.

"What the hell have you done to yourself?" Devon asked in disgust.

Rafael opened one eye and squinted, then made a shooing gesture with his hand. "Get the hell out of my apartment."

"You're shit-faced."

"I always said you were the smart one in this partnership."

"Mind telling me what prompted you to tie one on when you should be salvaging a business deal you seem determined to flush down the toilet?"

"I don't give a damn about the resort. Or you. Or anyone else. Get lost."

Rafael closed his eye again and reached for the bottle he'd left on the floor by the couch. Damn thing was empty. His mouth felt like he'd ingested a bag of cotton balls and his head ached like a son of a bitch.

Suddenly he was jerked off the couch, hauled

across the floor and slammed into one of the armchairs. He opened his eyes again to see Devon's
snarling face just inches from his own.

"You're going to tell me what the hell is going
on here," Devon demanded. "Cam said everything was fine when he picked you up. Then suddenly you go radio silent and I come up here to
check on your ass and you're so liquored up you
can't see straight."

Pain splintered Rafael's chest, and worse,
shame crowded in from every direction. He'd
never been so ashamed in his life.

"I'm a bastard," he said hoarsely.

Devon snorted. "Yeah, well, what else is new?
It never bothered you before."

Rafael lunged to his feet, gathered Devon's shirt
in his fists and got into Devon's face. "Maybe it
bothers me *now*. Damn it, Devon, I remember everything, okay? Every single detail and it makes
me so sick I can't even think about it."

Devon's eyes narrowed but he made no move
to remove Rafael's hands from his shirt. "What
the hell are you talking about? What do you remember that's so bad?"

"I used her," Rafael said quietly. "I went down
there with the sole intention of doing whatever

it took to get the land. And I did. God, I did. I seduced her. I told her I loved her. I promised her whatever she wanted to hear. All so I could make this deal happen. And it was all a lie. I left there with the intention of never going back. I had what I wanted. The sale was closed. The paperwork was filed. I had won."

A wounded cry from the doorway made Rafael jerk his head around. He went numb from head to toe when he saw Bryony standing there, white as a sheet, Ryan right beside her, supporting her with an arm when she'd stumbled back.

It was a nightmare. His worst nightmare come to life. What was she doing here? Why now?

He let go of Devon's shirt and started toward her. "Bryony." Her name spilled from his lips, a tortured sound that reflected all the shame and guilt that crowded his soul.

She took a hasty step back, shaking off Ryan's arm. She was so pale that he worried she'd fall right over.

"Bryony, please, just listen to me."

She shook her head, tears filling her beautiful eyes. It was a sight that staggered him.

"Please, just leave me alone," she begged softly. "Don't say anything else. There isn't a need. I heard it all. Leave me with some of my pride at least."

She turned and fled into the elevator, the sound of her quiet sobs echoing through his apartment.

Rafael stood, feeling dead on the inside as he watched the elevator close. "Go after her," he croaked out to Ryan. "Please, for me. Make sure she's okay. She doesn't know anyone here in the city. I don't want anything to happen to her."

With a curse, Ryan turned and jammed his finger over the call button. Behind Rafael, Devon got on the phone and called down to the doorman with muttered instructions to stall Bryony until Ryan arrived.

"Why aren't you going after her yourself?" Devon asked after Ryan got into the returning elevator.

Rafael dropped back into the armchair and cupped his head between both hands. "What am I supposed to say to her? I lied to her. I played her. I used her. Everything she feared I had done, I absolutely did."

Devon sat on the edge of the couch and eyed his friend. "And now?"

"I love her. And knowing what I did to her, what I felt while I was doing it, sickens me. I'm so ashamed of the person I was that I can't even think about it without wanting to puke."

"No one says you have to be that person now," Devon said quietly.

Rafael closed his eyes and shook his head. "Do you know she's been telling me that all along? She kept saying that I didn't have to be the person I always was and that just because something has always been didn't mean it always had to be."

"Sounds like a smart woman."

"Oh, God, Devon, I messed this up. How could I have done what I did? How could I have done something like that to her? She's the most beautiful, loving and generous woman I've ever met. She's everything I've ever wanted. Her and our child. I want us to be a family. But how can she ever forgive me for this? How can I ever forgive myself?"

"I don't have the answers," Devon admitted. "But you won't find them here. You're going to have to fight for her if you love her and want her. If you give up, that just tells her that you are the man you used to be and that you haven't changed."

Rafael raised his head, his chest so heavy that it was a physical ache. "I can't let her go. I have no idea how I'm going to make her understand, but I can't let her go. No matter what I did then, no matter how big of a bastard I was then, that's not who I am now. I love her. I want another chance. God, if she'll just give me another chance, I'll never give her reason to doubt me again."

"You're convincing the wrong person," Devon said. "I'm on your side, man. Even if you are the biggest jackass in North America. And hey, whatever happens with this resort deal, I'm behind you one-hundred percent, okay? We'll figure something out. Now go get your girl."

Twenty-One

Bryony walked off the elevator in shock. Her limbs were numb. Her hands were like ice. She was on autopilot, her mind barely functioning.

Rafael's harsh words played over and over in her mind.

I used her.

I seduced her.

She flinched and wobbled toward the door, where the doorman stepped in front of her and put a hand on her arm. "Miss Morgan, if you would wait here, please."

She looked up at the man in confusion. "Why?"

"Just wait, please."

She shook her head and started to walk out the

door only to have him take her arm and steer her back into the lobby again.

Anger was slowly replacing her numb shock. She yanked her arm away from the older man and retreated. "Don't touch me." She backed right into another person; she turned to excuse herself but found herself looking up at the mountain who worked as Rafael's head of security.

"Miss Morgan, I had no idea you were in the city." He frowned. "You should have let Mr. de Luca know so I could have met you at the airport. Did you come with no escort?"

The doorman looked relieved that Ramon was there and he hastily resumed his position by the door, leaving her to stand by the security man.

"I'm not staying," she said tightly. "In fact, I'm on my way back to the airport now."

Ramon looked puzzled, and then Ryan Beardsley was there, inserting himself between her and Ramon.

"That will be all, Ramon. I'll take Miss Morgan where she needs to go."

"The hell you will," Bryony muttered. She turned and stalked toward the door.

Ryan caught up to her as soon as she stepped outside. He took her arm, but his hold was gentle.

So was the look on his face. The sympathy burning in his eyes made her want to cry.

"Let me give you a ride," he offered gently. "It's cold and you really shouldn't take a cab if you have no idea where you're going. You probably don't even have a hotel, am I right?"

She shook her head. "I was planning to stay with Rafael." She broke off as tears brimmed in her eyes.

"Come on," he said. "I'll take you to my place. It's not far. I have a spare bedroom."

"I want to go back to the airport," she said. "There's no point in staying here."

He hesitated and then cupped her elbow to lead her out of the building. "All right. I'll take you back to the airport. But I'm not leaving you until you get on a plane. You probably haven't even eaten anything, have you?"

She looked at him, utterly confused by how nice he was being to her.

"Why are you doing this?" she asked.

He stared at her for a long moment, brief pain flickering in his own eyes. "Because I know what it's like to have the rug completely pulled out from under you. I know what it's like to find out something about someone you cared about. I know what it's like to be lied to."

Her shoulders sagged and she wiped a shaking hand through her hair. "I'm just going to cry all over you."

His smile was brief but he turned her and motioned to a distant car. "You can cry all you want to. From what I heard, you're entitled."

"You can go now," Bryony said in a low voice, as Ryan hoisted her only bag onto the scale at the airline check-in desk.

"You've got a little time. Let's go get something to eat. You're pale and you're shaking still."

"I don't think I can." She placed her hand on her stomach and tried to will the queasiness away.

"Then a drink. Some juice. I'll make sure you get back to security in enough time to catch your flight."

She sighed her acceptance. It was much easier to just cede to Ryan's determination, though for the life of her she couldn't figure it out. In a few moments he had her seated at a little round table outside a tiny bistro, a tall glass of orange juice in front of her.

Her eyes watered as she stared sightlessly at

it. Her fingers trembled as she touched the cool surface.

"Ah, hell, you aren't going to cry again, are you?"

She sucked in steadying breaths. "I'm sorry. You've been nothing but kind. You don't deserve to have me fall apart all over you."

"It's okay. I understand how you feel."

"Oh?" she asked in a shaky voice. "You said you knew what it felt like. Who screwed you over?"

"The woman I was supposed to marry."

She winced. "Ouch. Yeah, it sucks, doesn't it? At least Rafael never promised to marry me. He certainly hinted about it but he never went that far in his deception. So what happened?"

Ryan's mouth twisted and for a moment, Bryony thought he'd say nothing.

"She slept with my brother just weeks after we became engaged."

"That'll do it," she said wearily. "I'm sorry that happened to you. Sucks when people you put all your faith into gut you in return."

"That about sums up my feelings on the subject," Ryan said with an amused chuckle.

She drained the juice and set the glass back down on the table.

"Let me get you something to eat. Can you keep it down now?"

Ryan's concern was endearing and she offered a halfhearted smile. "Thanks. I don't feel hungry, but you're right. I should probably eat."

He got up and a few minutes later returned with a selection of deli sandwiches and another glass of orange juice. As soon as she took the first bite, she realized just how hungry she was.

Ryan studied her for a long moment, sympathy bright in his eyes. "What will you do now?"

She paused midchew and then continued before swallowing. She took a sip of the juice and then set the glass back down.

"Go home. Have a baby. Try to forget. Move on with my life. I have my grandmother and the people on the island. I'll be fine."

"I wonder if that's what Kelly did," he mused aloud. "Went on with her life."

"Is that her name? Kelly? Your ex-fiancée?"

He nodded.

"So she didn't hang around? With your brother I mean? I suppose that would be awkward at family get-togethers."

"No, she didn't hang around. I have no idea where she went."

"Probably just as well. If she was the kind of person who'd sleep with the brother of the man she's going to marry, she isn't worth your idle curiosity."

"Maybe," he said quietly.

Silence fell and Bryony picked at her food, getting down what she could. She kept hearing Rafael's damning words over and over in her head. No matter what she did, she couldn't turn it off, couldn't make it go away.

She was humiliated. She was angry. But more than anything, she was destroyed. Twice she'd allowed him to manipulate her and to make her love him. Worse, she'd fallen even deeper in love the second time around. She'd been ready to capitulate and give him what he'd wanted all along. What he didn't even *need* from her because he had no intention of ever honoring his promise to her.

She was twice a fool for believing him and for not being smart enough to get the agreement in writing.

She was an even bigger fool for loving him.

A tear slid down her cheek and she hastily

wiped it away but to her dismay another fell in its place.

"I'm sorry, Bryony. You didn't deserve this," Ryan said quietly. "Rafael is my friend, but he went too far. I'm sorry you got caught in the middle of this deal."

She wiped away more tears and bowed her head. "I'm sorry, too. I wanted so much for it all to be real even when my head knew that something wasn't right. I should have never come to New York to confront him. I should have trusted my first instinct. He used me to get what he wanted. I knew that and I couldn't leave it alone. If I had just stayed home, I'd be over it by now and I would have never gotten involved with him a second time."

"Would you be over it?" Ryan asked gently.

"I don't know. Maybe… I definitely wouldn't be sitting here crying my eyes out, thousands of miles from home."

"True," Ryan conceded. He checked his watch and grimaced. "We should get you to security. Your flight leaves soon." His phone rang, and he looked down then frowned. He hesitated a moment and then punched a button to silence the ring. Then he looked back up. "You ready?"

She nodded. "Thank you, Ryan. Really. You didn't have to be this nice. I appreciate it."

Ryan smiled as he took her arm and they began the walk toward the security line. When they reached the end, she turned and blew out a deep breath. "Okay, well, this is it."

Ryan touched her cheek and then to her surprise pulled her into his arms for a tight hug.

"You take care of yourself and that baby," he said gruffly.

She pulled away and smiled up at him. "Thanks."

Squaring her shoulders, she eased into the security line. In a few hours she'd be back home.

Twenty-Two

Rafael dragged himself into the shower, washed the remnants of his alcohol binge from his fuzzy brain and proceeded to punish himself with fifteen minutes of ice-cold water. He'd been trying to call Ryan to find out where the hell Bryony was, but Ryan wasn't answering. He had to get his act together and prepare to plead his case to her. This was the most important deal of his life. Not the resort. Not the potential merger with Copeland Hotels. Not his partnership with his friends.

Bryony and their child were more important than any of that. He was furious that he could have been such a cold, calculating bastard with her before. But if she'd listen to him, if she'd just give him another chance, he'd prove to her that nothing in this world was more important to him than her.

By the time he got out, his mind was clear, he was freezing his ass off and he had only one clear purpose. Get Bryony back.

He dressed and strode into the living room, surprised to see Devon and Cam both sprawled in the armchairs.

"You two look like hell," he commented on his way to the kitchen.

Cam snorted. "You're one to talk, alcohol boy. When was the last time you went on a bender like that? Weren't we in college? Hasn't anyone told you we're too old for stuff like that now? It's a good way to poison yourself."

"Tell me something I don't know," Rafael muttered.

"So what's the plan?" Devon drawled.

"I've got to get her back," Rafael said. "Screw the deal. Screw the resort. This is my life. The woman I love. My child. I can't give them up over some ridiculous development deal."

"You're serious," Cam said.

"Of course I'm serious," Rafael snarled. "I'm

not the same bastard who would do anything at all to close a deal. I don't *want* to be that man any longer. I don't know how you stood him for as long as you did."

Cam grinned. "Well, okay then. Don't get pissy about it."

"Have either of you heard from Ryan? I sent him after her, but the son of a bitch won't answer his phone."

Devon shook his head. "I'll try him. Maybe he's just not answering *your* calls."

Like that was supposed to make Rafael feel any better. But at this point, he didn't care how he had to get to Bryony. Just as long as he did.

Just as Devon put the phone to his ear, the elevator doors chimed and Rafael jerked around, holding his breath that by some miracle Bryony had come back. He let it all out when he saw Ryan stride in.

Rafael strode forward to meet him. "Where the hell is Bryony? I've been calling you for the last couple of hours. Where have you been?"

Ryan glared back. There was condemnation in his eyes. And anger. "I just spent the past couple of hours listening to Bryony cry because you broke her heart. I hope to hell you're happy now that you've destroyed the best thing that's ever happened to you."

"Whoa, back off," Devon said as he stood. "This isn't any of our business, Ryan. He's already beaten himself up enough without you piling on."

"Yeah, well, you didn't have to listen to her cry."

"Where is she?" Rafael demanded when he found his voice. The image of Bryony crying sent staggering pain through his chest. "I need to see her, Ryan. Where did you take her?"

"To the airport."

Rafael's heart dropped. "The airport? Has she already left? Do I have time to catch her?"

Ryan shook his head. "She's probably already in the air."

Rafael cursed. Then he turned and slammed his fist into the wall. He leaned his forehead against the cabinet and fought the rage that billowed inside him.

When he looked up, an odd sort of peace settled over him. He looked at his friends—his business partners—and knew that this could very well be the end of their relationship.

"I have to go after her," he said.

Devon nodded. "Yeah, you do."

"I'm canceling the deal. I'm pulling the plug. I don't give a damn how much it costs me or if it costs me *everything*. It already has. I'm going to give back that damn land. Bryony will never believe that I love her as long as it stands between us. I have to get rid of it and make it a nonissue."

Slowly Cam nodded. "I agree. It's the only way you're going to get her to believe that you love her now."

To his surprise, all three of his friends nodded their agreement.

"You're not pissed? We had a lot riding on this."

"How about you let us deal with the resort plans," Devon said. "You go after your woman. Settle down. Have babies. Be nauseatingly happy. I'm going to see what I can do to salvage the resort proposal. Maybe we can find another location."

"I'm not even going to ask," Rafael said. "Tell me about it later. I owe you. I owe you big."

"Yeah, well, don't think I won't collect. Later. After you've kissed and made up with Bryony," Devon said with a grin.

"Need a ride to the airport?" Ryan asked.

"My driver's still outside. I told him I wouldn't be long."

"Yeah. Just let me get my wallet."

"Not going to pack a bag?" Cam asked.

"Hell, no. Bryony can buy me more jeans and flip-flops when I get down there."

"After she kicks your ass you mean?" Devon asked.

"I'll let her do whatever she wants just as long as she takes me back," Rafael said.

"Good God," Cam said in disgust. "Could you sound any more pathetic?"

Devon laughed and slapped Cam on the back. "Apparently that's what falling in love does to a guy. Take my advice. Marry for money and connections, like I am."

"I think the best idea is to never marry," Cam pointed out. "Less expensive that way. No costly divorces."

Rafael shook his head. "And you all called me the bastard. Come on, Ryan. I've got a plane to catch."

"Bryony!"

Bryony turned to see her grandmother waving to

her from her deck. Silas stood beside her, watching as Bryony stood close to the water's edge.

She'd been there for a couple of hours, just watching the water, alone with her thoughts. She knew her grandmother and Silas were both worried. She'd given them an abbreviated version of everything that had happened. No sense in them knowing the extent of Bryony's stupidity.

They knew enough that Rafael had made a fool of her and would develop the land, but then Bryony had been prepared to give up that fight. So the outcome would be the same, only Bryony wouldn't have the man she loved.

Bryony waved but turned back to the water, not ready to deal with them yet. Mamaw and Silas had both fussed over her ever since she'd gotten back home. She was exhausted and what she really wanted was to go to sleep for about twenty-four hours, but every time she closed her eyes, she heard Rafael's words. They wouldn't go away, she couldn't make herself stop hearing them no matter how hard she tried.

And she was damn tired of crying. Her head ached so badly from all the tears she'd shed that it was ready to explode.

Her cell phone rang in her pocket and she

picked it up, just as she'd done the other twenty times that Rafael had tried to call her. She hit the ignore button and a few seconds later, heard the ding signaling that she had a voice mail. One of the many he'd left her.

What else was there left for him to say? He was sorry? He hadn't meant to deceive her? Was she supposed to forgive him just because he forgot what a jerk he had been? How could she be sure he hadn't made it all up just to get her to shut up and not make noises that would scare off his precious investors?

If he kept her quiet enough for long enough then the deal would be sealed.

She didn't like how cynical she'd grown. It would never occur to her before that anyone would be so devious, but Rafael had taught her a lot about the world of business and the lengths that some people would go for money.

She hoped he made a ton off his precious resort and she hoped it kept him warm at night. She hoped it made up for all the sweet baby kisses he'd miss.

The thought depressed her. Money was just paper. But a child was something so very precious. Love was precious. And she'd offered it to Rafael freely and without reservation.

She felt like the worst sort of naive fool.

Finally her feet got cold enough from the surf that she could no longer feel her toes, so she turned to trudge back up to her grandmother's deck. She'd say her goodbyes, assure Mamaw that she'd be just fine and then she'd go home and hopefully sleep for the next day.

As she got close, she saw Rafael standing on the deck and Mamaw and Silas were nowhere to be found. How the hell had he gotten down here so fast? Why would he even bother? She didn't react to his presence. She wouldn't give him the satisfaction.

She walked up the steps, past him to collect her sweater and then she started down the walkway that led to her own cottage.

"Bryony," he called after her. "Wait, please. We have to talk."

She picked up her pace. She knew he followed her because she could hear his footsteps behind her, but she blindly went on. When she reached to open her door, his hand closed around her wrist and gently pulled her away.

"Please listen to me," he begged softly. "I know

I don't deserve anything from you. But please listen. I love you."

She went rigid and closed her eyes as pain crashed over her all over again. When she re-opened them she was grateful that no tears spilled over her cheeks. Maybe she'd finally cried herself out.

"You don't know how to love," she said in a low voice. "You have to possess a heart and a soul, and you have neither."

He winced but didn't let go of her wrist. "I'm not going to lie to you, Bryony. Neither am I going to sugarcoat what I did."

"Well, good for you," she said bitterly. "Does that ease your conscience? Just leave me alone, Rafael. You got what you wanted. You don't have to deal with me anymore. Just make this easier on both of us. If you're wanting absolution, see a priest. I can't offer you any. You should be happy. You got the land. You'll build your resort. Every-one gets what they want."

"Not you," he said painfully. "And not me."

"Please, Rafael," she begged. "I'm tired. I'm worn completely out. I just want to sleep before I fall over. Please, just go. I can't do this with you right now."

He looked so much like he wanted to argue, but concern darkened his eyes and slowly he eased his fingers from her wrist.

"I love you, Bryony. That's not going to change. I don't want it to change. Go get some sleep. Take care of yourself. But this isn't finished. I'm not letting you go. You think I'm ruthless? You haven't seen anything yet."

He touched her cheek and then let it slide down her face before falling away. Then he turned and walked back down the path to her grandmother's house.

She closed her eyes as pain swelled in her chest and splintered in a thousand different directions. She wanted to scream. She wanted to cry. But all she could do was stand there numbly while the man she'd given everything to walked away.

Twenty-Three

"It's been a week," Rafael said in frustration. "A week and she still won't acknowledge me, much less talk to me. As much as I loathe the man I used to be, at least he would have no qualms about forcing the issue."

Rafael stood on Laura's back deck having a beer with Silas and brooded over the fact that Bryony still refused to see him. He was about to go crazy.

Silas chuckled. "You've got stamina, son. I have to give that to you. Most men would have tucked tail and left by now. I'm still amazed that you managed to talk Laura down from killing you and actually got her to side with you. I can't figure out if you're the dumbest man alive or just the luckiest."

Bryony had holed up in her cottage and while Laura went over daily to check in on her, Bryony hadn't ventured out except to walk on the beach. The one time Rafael had confronted her on the sand, she'd retreated inside. He hadn't bothered her since because he wanted her to have that time outside without worrying that she'd encounter him.

"I'm not leaving," Rafael said. "I don't care how long it takes. I love her. I believe she still loves me, but she's hurting. I can't even blame her for that. I was a complete and utter bastard. I don't deserve her but she's the one who kept telling me I didn't have to be the same man. Well, damn it, I'm choosing to be different. I want her to see that."

Silas put his hand on Rafael's shoulder. "Around here we have a saying. Go big or go home. I'm thinking you need to go big. Really big."

Rafael frowned and turned to the other man. "What did you have in mind?"

"It's not what I have in mind. It's what you ought to be thinking about. You've already promised me and Laura that you have no intention of developing that land, but does she know that? Does the rest of the island know that? Seems to me you're missing an opportunity to make a grand gesture and prove once and for all you're a changed man."

"Okay, I'm with you," Rafael said slowly.

"No, I don't think you are. Call a town meeting. I'll let it leak out that you have a big announcement about the resort. Folks will show up because they'll want to launch their objections and nothing gets people out to a town meeting more than getting to air their grievances. Trust me, after twenty years of being the sheriff here, I know what I'm talking about."

"That doesn't help me when Bryony refuses to leave her cottage," Rafael pointed out.

"Oh, Laura and I will make sure she's there. You just worry about how you're going to humble yourself before everyone," Silas said with a grin.

Rafael sighed. He had the feeling this wasn't going to be one of his better moments. He might have no desire to be the unfeeling bastard he'd been before but it didn't mean he wanted to air his personal life in front of a few hundred witnesses.

But if it would get him in front of Bryony so she'd be forced to listen, he'd swallow his pride and do it.

"Are you crazy?" Bryony sputtered out. "Why would I want to go listen to his spiel about his plans for the resort?"

"Now, Bry, I didn't imagine you for a coward," Silas said in exasperation. "By now everyone knows what happened. They don't blame you."

"I don't care what they think," Bryony said in a low voice. "I was prepared to be the brunt of their censure when I went to New York to tell Rafael to go ahead with the plans, that I wouldn't fight him."

"Then what's the problem?" Mamaw asked.

"I don't want to see him. Why can't either of you understand that? Do you have any idea how much it hurts to even look at him?"

"The best thing you can do is show up with your head held high. The sooner you get it over with, the sooner you can start coming out of that cottage of yours. It's just like a bandage. Better to rip it off and have it done with than to delay the inevitable."

Bryony sighed. "Okay, I'll go. If I do, then will

you please leave me alone and let me deal with this my own way? I know you're worried but this isn't easy for me."

Mamaw squeezed her into a big hug. "I think things will be a lot better after today. You'll see."

Bryony wasn't as convinced but she allowed Silas and Mamaw to drag her to the municipal building where the meeting would be held. It took everything she had not to run back out the door when Silas led her to a front-row seat.

Talk about being a masochist. She'd have a front-row seat in which to listen to the man she loved announce his plans for a resort made possible by her stupidity.

She sighed and sank into one of the folding chairs. Mamaw and Silas took the spots on either side of her. Several people stopped by to talk to Silas. Some even shot sympathetic looks in her direction.

Yep, it was clear everyone knew what a naive fool she'd been.

At least no one was yelling at her for allowing the outsider to come in and develop the island. Yet.

Rupert strode in a minute later, an uncharacteristic smile plastered on his face. It wasn't his politician smile. It was a genuine one filled with delight. He looked, for lack of a better word, giddy.

He held up his hands for quiet and then frowned when the din didn't diminish. He cleared his throat and scowled harder. He was forever complaining to Bryony that he wasn't given enough respect by his constituents.

Finally Silas stood, held up his hands and hollered, "Quiet, people. The mayor wants your attention."

Rupert sent Silas a disgruntled look when everyone hushed. Then he looked over the audience and smiled. "Today we have Rafael de Luca of Tricorp Investment Opportunities, who is going to talk about the piece of property he recently acquired here on the island. Give him your undivided attention, please."

It took all of Bryony's self-restraint not to swivel in her seat to see if he was here. Many of the assembled people began to murmur, and then Bryony heard footsteps coming up the aisle.

Rafael stepped to the podium and Bryony was shocked by his appearance. First, he was wearing jeans. And a T-shirt. He looked tired and haggard. His hair was unkempt and it didn't look like he'd shaved that morning.

There were hollows under his eyes and a gray pallor to his skin that hadn't been present before.

He cleared his throat and glanced over the audience before his gaze finally came to rest on her.

He looked…nervous. It didn't seem possible that this ultraconfident businessman was nervous. But he seemed uneasy and on edge.

She watched in astonishment as he fiddled with something on the podium and when he looked up again, there was a rawness to his eyes that made her chest tighten.

"I came to this island for one thing and one thing only. I wanted to buy property that Bryony Morgan had put up for sale."

Several muttered insults filtered around the room, but Rafael continued on, undaunted.

"When it became clear that she would attach stipulations to the sale of the land, I conspired to seduce my way into her heart. Basically I was willing to do whatever necessary to convince her I'd do as she asked without having to commit her conditions onto paper."

Bryony would have bolted to her feet, but Mamaw gripped her arm with surprising strength.

"Sit. You need to listen to this, Bryony. Let him finish."

Rafael held up his hands to quiet the angry murmurs of the crowd. Then his gaze found Bryony's again. She slowly slid back into her seat, caught by the intensity in his stare.

"I'm not proud of what I did. But it was part and parcel of the kind of man I was. I left here, never intending to return until it was time for groundbreaking. But my plane crashed. It took weeks to recover and I lost all memory of the time I was here. I'm so grateful for that accident. It changed my life."

The room went completely silent on the heels of his last statement. Everyone seemed to lean forward in anticipation of what he'd say next.

"I came back here with Bryony to try to regain my memory. What I did was fall in love with this island and with Bryony. For real this time. She's told me on multiple occasions that I don't have to always stay the person I was, that I can change and be whoever I want to be. She's right. I don't want to be the person I was any longer. I want to be someone I can be proud of, someone *she* can be proud of. I want to be the man Bryony Morgan loves."

Tears crowded Bryony's eyes and her fingers curled into tight little fists in her lap. Mamaw reached over to take one of her hands and rubbed it reassuringly.

"I'm giving Bryony back the land I bought from her. It's hers to do as she likes. If she wishes, she can make it a gift and deed it to the town. Turn it into a park. Make it a private sanctuary. I don't care. Because all I want is her. And our child."

He stopped speaking and seemed to be battling to keep his composure. His fingers curled around the edges of the podium, but she could see that they still shook.

Then he walked around the podium, down the single step that elevated the stage. He came to a stop in front of her and then dropped to one knee. He reached for her hand and gently pried her fingers open and then he laced them with his, something he'd done a hundred times before.

"I love you, Bryony. Forgive me. Marry me. Say you'll make me a better man than I was. I'll spend the rest of my life *being* that man for you and our children."

A sob exploded from her throat at the same moment she launched herself from her seat and threw her arms around him. She buried her face in his neck and sobbed huge, noisy sobs.

He gripped her tight, holding one hand to the back of her head. He shook against her, almost as if he were dangerously close to breaking down himself.

He kissed her ear, her temple, her forehead, the top of her head. Then he pulled back, framing her face in his hands before peppering the rest of it with kisses.

Around them there were sighs and exclamations, even a smattering of applause, but Bryony tuned them all out as she held on to the one thing she needed most in this world.

Rafael.

"Give me your answer, please, baby," he murmured in her ear. "Don't torture me any longer. Tell me I haven't lost you for good. I can be the man you want, Bryony. Just give me the chance."

She kissed him and stroked her hands over his face, feeling the stubble on his jaw and drinking in the haggardness of his appearance. He looked as bad as she'd felt over the past week.

"You already are the man I want, Rafael. I love you. Yes, I'll marry you."

He shot to his feet and lifted her up, twirling her round and round with a whoop. "She said yes!"

The crowd burst into cheers. Mamaw sniffed indelicately and when Silas handed her a handkerchief, she blew her nose loudly and then sniffed some more.

Slowly he allowed her to slide down his body until her feet touched the floor, but he kept his arms tight around her as if he didn't want to let her go even for a moment.

"I'm sorry, Bryony," he said sincerely. "I'm sorry I lied to you, that I hurt you. If I could go back and change it all I would."

"I'm glad you can't," she said. "As I sat here and listened to everything you said, I realized that if things hadn't happened exactly as they had, you wouldn't be here now. What's important is that you love me now. Today. And tomorrow."

"I'll love you through lots of tomorrows," he vowed.

Bryony glanced around as the townspeople began filtering out of the building. Mamaw and Silas had discreetly made their exit, leaving Bryony and Rafael alone at the front of the room.

"What are we going to do, Rafe? What are you going to do? I came to New York because I was going to tell you that you should go ahead with the resort deal. But if you don't go through with it, what will it mean for your business?"

Rafael sighed. "Ryan, Devon and Cam support me. You support me. That's all I need. When I left, they were trying to work out a way to salvage the deal. I'm guessing they'll look for an alternative location. I really don't care. I told them I wasn't going to lose you and my child over money. You and our baby mean more to me than anything else in the world. I mean that."

"After the spectacle you just made of yourself, I believe you," she teased.

"I'm tired," he admitted. "And so are you. Why don't we go back to your cottage, climb into bed and get some rest. I can't think of anything better than having you back in my arms."

She leaned into his embrace, wrapped her arms around him and closed her eyes as the sweetness of the moment floated gently through her veins.

Then she tilted her head back and smiled up at him, feeling the weight and grief wash away. For the first time in days, the thick blanket of sadness lifted, leaving her feeling light and gloriously happy.

She took his hand and tugged him down the

aisle to the doorway leading to the outside. As they stepped out, sunlight poured over them, washing the darkness away.

For a brief moment, she paused and tipped her face into the sun, allowing the warmth to brush over her cheeks.

She looked up at Rafael, who was staring intently at her. His love was there for the entire world to see, shining in his eyes with brightness that rivaled the sun.

It was a look she'd never grow tired of in a hundred years and beyond.

"Let's go home," she said.

Rafael smiled, took her hand and pulled her toward the waiting car.

* * * * *